THE STEAM CHASERS: WE MADE THAT

By Dr. Doresa A. Jennings

Dr. Doresa A. Jennings

Book #1

We Made That!

For all the kids who ever wondered if the world would make room for them and their dreams.

Love Always, Doresa

A special thank you to all of my supporters on Kickstarter who made sure this book became a reality. Your belief in the importance of this work will always move me. Your trust in my ability to tell this much needed story in the appropriate way continues to motivate me. Your confidence that this is just the first of many STEAM Chasers books keeps me writing daily to ensure this series moves – Full STEAM Ahead!

Special thank you to cover illustrator TheCMDStudios for bringing Shar, Terrence, Ebony, Akiya, Marcus, and Chase to life!

Thank you isn't enough for the support, encouragement, and patience provided to me by my husband Keelan and real life STEAM Chasing children Javon, Jordan, and Makaila. Thank you for constant support.

This book is a work of fiction. Any references to historical events, real people, or real locations are used fictitiously. Other names, characters, places, and incidents are the product of the author's imagination, and any resemblance to actual events or locals or persons is entirely coincidental.

Doresa Ayanna Publications
DoresaAyanna.com

ISBN: 978-1-951054-00-7

Table of Contents

Chapter One

"Two points if I make it!" Chase shouted to Marcus as he was squaring his shoulders and standing with his half full milk carton in his hand. As usual, he had drawn the attention of most of the students in the cafeteria. Most people began smiling in anticipation of just what Chase might do this time. He and his cousin, Marcus, were the most famous sixth graders in the school for their ability to *almost* break the rules in the most exciting of ways. They never did anything that would get them into major trouble, but that didn't mean a bit of minor trouble was out of the question.

"No way, you're too close! If you want two points, you need to back way up." Marcus was pointing to a spot about four feet back from where Chase was standing.

The cafeteria was loud, as usual. However, when everyone saw Chase lining up for his shot, they stopped talking just a bit to see what he was up to. Terrence got up to approach Chase. “Do you really think this is a good idea?” Terrence was usually the voice of reason for the two cousins. A voice they had an uncanny ability to ignore.

“I mean it might not be the best idea I’ve had. I think a better one would be to use something like a gallon of milk, but that is a serious waste of food. You know, I’m all about conservation.” Chase laughed as he lined up his shot.

“Come on, Jiminy Cricket,” teased Marcus. “Let the man live a little.” As more eyes in the cafeteria diverted to Chase, Marcus made sure to gesture to them that they were in for a good show.

“He’s going to be living in detention for the rest of his life, with you sitting next to him.” Shar was walking past the boys to throw away her trash.

"This school doesn't even have detention!" shouted Marcus, sounding triumphant in knowing something Shar didn't.

Ebony chimed in, "I think they might be willing to make an exception for you two." She shook her head disapprovingly as she walked past and caught up with Shar heading back to their table after they'd dumped their garbage.

"I hear they already started building a dungeon. You know, to contain the lightning and thunder." Akiya laughed loudly. While she walked with Shar and Ebony, she still managed to get a peek at Chase with what he could tell was an interest in what he would do next.

"Ha!" shouted Chase, still cautiously lining up his shot. "I laugh in the face of those who would try to bind my awesomeness. Now behold, young ones, and watch PERFECTION!" With that, he jumped up and released the carton of milk. It went straight up about eight feet in the air and then curved to sail toward the garbage can. It looked like he just might make it.

"Looks like someone should have spent more time studying physics and less time working on his victory speech. You know, until he actually had the victory." Ebony smirked and headed toward the exit. Shar and Akiya walked past as well, both avoiding the now spilled milk in an exaggerated manner.

"No points! Better luck next time," said Marcus as he turned to walk away. He didn't make it far, as he immediately bumped into Principal Davis, who was holding a mop and a bucket of water.

"Well, you two, I'll let Mrs. Worthington know you're going to be a little late." He handed the mop to Chase and the bucket to Marcus. Principal Davis was wearing his usual attire of a black suit, white shirt, and perfectly polished shoes. At six feet and four inches tall, he could easily strike fear into the hearts of any kids. He seemed to understand how imposing his dark eyes could be, so he mostly led conversations with a smile and always managed to wear a themed tie. Today's tie was filled with cupcakes topped with pink or brown frosting. Each cupcake was sporting one candle and each candle had a flame that must have been powered by tiny LED lights because they were blinking. It was kind of hard to be completely afraid of someone who thought it was a good idea to wear flashing birthday candles, even if they stood over a foot taller than you.

"It shouldn't take that long to clean up. The carton was mostly empty. We'll be done in no time," answered Chase, who thought an entire pail of soapy water was a bit of overkill for a little spilled milk. It would seem a couple of paper towels would have worked just fine.

"Oh, you're not just cleaning up this spot. You two get the pleasure of mopping the entire cafeteria. I let Mr. Phil know you two would give him a hand in cleaning, since you were over contributing to the mess here today." Principal Davis had the uncanny ability to be firm and gentle at the same time.

"Wait, how did you even see all this? Were you watching the whole time?" asked Marcus.

“Yes, I was actually talking to Mr. Phil when Chase first started lining up his shot.” Principal Davis looked down at the boys with what they hoped was a genuine smile.

“Well, why didn’t you stop me?” asked Chase, putting the mop into the bucket of water. He couldn’t believe the principal actually let him go for that basket, knowing it could have resulted in a mess. He and Marcus were usually more careful about who was around when they performed one of their famous stunts.

“I always like to give students the opportunity to do the right thing on their own. I also like for you to learn to encourage each other to do the right thing all on your own.” With these words, Mr. Davis was looking directly at Terrence and giving an appreciative smile. “Since you couldn’t be persuaded with logic ahead of time, I figure a few minutes spent mopping up the messes of your classmates will help you get a feel for what it is like for Mr. Phil and how frustrating it can be to watch people make an unnecessary mess when you will likely be the one who has to clean it up."

Chase and Marcus both looked at Mr. Phil already busily wiping down tables. Mr. Phil hummed to himself as he cleaned away the remnants of sticky drinks that had been spilled and crumbs from sandwiches. He had been the janitor at the Global Academy since it had opened three years ago. The Global Academy was the first STEAM focused middle school in the city, and they had managed to hire what all the kids thought were the best adults in the world. It was a special school that drew kids from all over the city. They accumulated their faculty and staff from all over the city as well, with many of them being people who had already retired but who'd decided to come back to their careers to ensure the Global Academy got off to a great start. Mr. Phil was no exception. While he was quiet, he only showed signs of the slightest of temper when students made big messes without trying to clean them up. Unfortunately, Chase and Marcus had been on Mr. Phil's radar twice so far this school year. They winced as he got slightly closer to the trashcan with the spilled milk.

Chase spoke first. “Mr. Davis, can we have a bit more time so that we can clean off the rest of the tables as well as mopping the floor? We can stay late to finish up any work that we miss in class.”

“Yes, maybe we can give Mr. Phil a break for today and we can all start tomorrow as if this never happened,” added Marcus. Both boys felt a rush of guilt at the unintended consequences of their stunt. It seemed innocent at first and they really didn’t intend to put more work on Mr. Phil’s plate. They hoped this gesture would help him to see that they really didn’t have ill intentions. The two boys stayed silent as most of the other kids filed out of the cafeteria and headed back to their classes. They tried to smile and look calm knowing everyone was wondering just what Principal Davis had in store for them.

“I think that is a great idea,” said Principal Davis, his eyes bright. “Why don’t you two go tell him the good news? You head off to class so you won't be late, Terrence."

"Yes, sir," answered Terrence, gathering his backpack. He ran to catch up with the final group of kids that were lingering at the door trying to wait as long as possible to figure out what could be the final outcome for Marcus and Chase. They knew the two cousins were pretty good with getting out of trouble, but this time just might be different since Principal Davis had seen the whole thing.

Marcus and Chase cautiously approached Mr. Phil, who was working quietly and quickly. Mr. Phil was a large man. Not overweight, but his broad shoulders and overall build had all the kids speculating that he must have been a linebacker when he was younger. Come to find out, they were correct about him being a former athlete, just the wrong sport. Mr. Phil had spent over a decade playing professional hockey for the NHL. He was one of the biggest and most feared players of the game. Despite his reputation on the ice, he was never one to start fights and had never been labeled a 'goon.' He was a fan favorite but wanted a quiet life once he'd retired from hockey. Even though he hadn't played professional hockey for thirty years, his frame still held a lot of muscles. He didn't speak much and never complained about the messes students made, but they still couldn't help but feel a little intimidated by his sheer presence. Whenever he was near, they seemed to drop less things on the floor and be a bit neater with what they were doing.

"Mr. Phil," Marcus and Chase spoke almost in unison,"we're really sorry."

"I shouldn't have thrown that milk, I knew it could have spilled if I missed. I do want to say that I really did think I would make the shot though!" said Chase, who was apologizing but also trying to plead his case just a bit.

"Well, I was pretty sure he wouldn't make the shot, especially when I encouraged him to back up even further from the garbage can. So I knew what was going to happen." Marcus looked at Chase and tried not to laugh.

"The point is," interrupted Chase, "we know we were wrong and we're sorry. We want to make it up to you by not just mopping the floor but also cleaning off the tables and chairs."

Mr. Phil didn't have much of an expression as he looked at Marcus and Chase, although a slight smile did enter his face. "I really appreciate the offer. How about this, all three of us can do the cleaning? It will make the work go faster and I'll have a bit of company. Look, I'm not mad at you boys. You two are good kids. You just have to think a bit more before you act. It's okay to challenge each other and even show off a bit, just think to make sure it's the right time and place for it."

"Thanks!" said both boys at the same time.

"Where do we start?" asked Marcus.

"Go grab some towels from the back, we'll finish wiping the tables down first, then sweep and mop the floor," answered Mr. Phil.

“My mom is not going to believe I actually volunteered to do extra cleaning,” said Marcus, shaking his head.

“Well, don’t run home bragging about it, because then she’ll ask why you were doing any cafeteria cleaning in the first place,” answered Chase.

“I’ll just tell her because you were a bad shot.” Marcus laughed and pretended to duck.

“Hey, the sun was in my eyes and there was a northerly wind that I didn’t anticipate.” Chase was trying to look serious, but a smile was breaking through.

“Dude, we’re in a building.”

With that, both boys laughed and grabbed cleaning rags. Chase hadn’t anticipated having to clean the cafeteria that day, but it didn’t seem like it would be too bad after all.

Chapter Two

Terrence stopped quickly by his locker then headed to Mrs. Worthington's class. As he rounded the corner, he saw Principal Davis leaving her door.

"Have a good class." Principal Davis smiled as he passed Terrence. True to his word, the principal must have stopped by to tell Mrs. Worthington Marcus and Chase would be late. Terrence wondered how Principal Davis had gotten to her class so quickly. He pondered if Marcus and Chase were correct when they mused there must be hidden passages around the school, since Principal Davis seemed to be everywhere at the same time.

Just like the rest of the school, Mrs. Worthington's classroom was uniquely decorated. The walls reflected the nature of the subjects taught in the classroom—social studies, geography, and history. There was a border along the wall close to the ceiling with pictures depicting important historical events, everything from the lunar landing to the desegregation of public schools in the south. There were framed historical documents on the walls, including the Declaration of Independence and the Emancipation Proclamation. There were globes and maps of all shapes and sizes, like the AuthaGraph map that could magically fold into a three-dimensional globe. There were flags from around the world and photos of people, especially kids, from all different cultures and communities. The word, "Hello," greeted students in seventeen different languages as soon as they walked through the door. In fact, Mrs. Worthington had once said she wanted anyone from anywhere in the world to walk through her classroom door and feel right at home. It wasn't just the walls and decorations that made her classroom interesting, it was also the way the furniture was arranged. The classroom contained no individual desks. There were three round tables for collaborative work. Bean bags were on the floor so small groups could have discussions comfortably. A wooden buddy bench next to the bookshelf flanked a quiet reading corner. Everything about the room made the students feel like learning and sharing. Mrs. Worthington was the favorite teacher of every student who ever had her, even though she gave some of the toughest assignments in the school. Walking into class, Terrence realized today would be no different, Mrs. Worthington was standing at the board, writing up the details of what was sure to be an interesting but intensive project.

"I returned your papers along with feedback for your presentations on the contributions of Asians to the American experience. A special thank you to Seung and his family for sharing authentic Korean food and Mayuree for sharing authentic Thai food. Thank you to group two, which included Ryan, Abigail, and Tyrone, for teaching us greetings and to count to ten in Mandarin, Tagalong, and Hindi. You all did such wonderful jobs, really—the entire class did amazingly well. Don't forget to write out for each group what you enjoyed the most from the presentation, something new that you learned, and also an opportunity in which they could improve for the next presentation they give. Your constructive criticism is really doing wonders, thank you so much for helping each other to become more confident presenters." Mrs. Worthington was finishing up her recap when Marcus and Chase entered the classroom.

#

"Sorry we're late," said Chase, who paused when he saw Mrs. Worthington had been writing on the board.

"You haven't missed anything new, Chase," answered Mrs. Worthington who smiled towards the boys. Chase wondered if she could sense he was nervous and that is why she gave such a warm welcome. “Principal Davis let me know you two were helping out in the cafeteria and would be a little late. I was waiting for you both before getting started with our new assignment. Go ahead and join your group.”

Marcus and Chase met Terrence who was standing in the reading area, looking over their paper and presentation grade.

“How did we do?” asked Marcus, with only a slight hesitation in his voice.

“We did great!” Terrence was excited as he gave the other two boys a high five. “Areas for improvement were editing our papers a bit more thoroughly and making sure to always include the year of publication when citing sources. Mrs. Worthington even put in a note for how to cite a source when we don’t know the year it was published.”

“Citing sources in middle school, sometimes I wonder if college will be easier not harder than what we do here,” said Chase with a half smile spreading across his face.

"Well, if we are rocking like this, college will be a breeze." Terrence was fanning the air with the paper and all three boys were now snickering.

Mrs. Worthington was now standing in front of the board and getting everyone's attention. "Okay, class, we are going to continue with our assignment of how the various subgroups of people in the United States have helped to shape the country we have today. Our next group we are going to be studying is Black Americans. You can be broad in your search, examining the impact Black Americans have had in areas of politics, culture, entertainment, sports, medicine, or the impact on our everyday lives."

Rebecca, a girl with green eyes and ginger hair, and who loved all things history, was raising her hand to ask a question.

"Yes, Rebecca?" asked Mrs. Worthington.

"You used the term Black American, I thought the term was African American. Is there a specific word we are supposed to use?" Rebecca asked, seriousness in her voice.

"That is a great question, Rebecca. One that your group might want to study. I will tell you, that answer can change depending on what groups within the subculture you are referring to, and also, people can choose the name by which they would like to be referred. I tend to use the term Black American, mainly because this is the self-identification that I grew up with in my household. However, you will get no points taken off by using African American or any other respectful term that you find. The naming of communities of people might be something quite interesting to explore." As Mrs. Worthington finished speaking, everyone could see Rebecca was feverishly taking notes. Her love of history was bubbling over now as she found even more nooks and crannies to explore.

Mrs. Worthington continued with the assignment instructions. "We are going to make one additional change, to shake things up a bit. Each group did a wonderful job with their presentation, and you all work really well together. I am not going to break up the various trios, I think it is great to stick with a group of people you work well with. But that doesn't mean we can't stretch ourselves a little as well. So, you won't be working with just your trio. We are going to combine with one other trio. So, instead of working in groups of three, you are going to be working in groups of six. Go ahead and start in your trio, then find another trio to partner with. You will be working as one group and will earn one grade. Yes, it will be more challenging writing a paper with six people instead of three and doing a presentation with six people instead of three. However, you will also notice that, as you add people, you add diversity of ideas and opinions and you should see a stronger final product in the end."

Akiya, Shar, and Ebony had been in the reading area looking over their grade when Mrs. Worthington mentioned joining with another trio. Shar began first. "We have done so well on every assignment. The biggest thing Mrs. Worthington asked us to work on was expanding ourselves a bit with our presentation. Our paper was well written with good research, but she thought we could go outside the box a bit when we presented our findings."

"I wonder what would be the best trio for us to join with? It would definitely make sense to work with a group that can help us be a bit more creative in the presentation department." Ebony spoke as she looked around the room.

"Well," said Akiya, almost hesitantly, "there is one group that has creativity pretty much on lock down."

"No way!" Shar yelled a little more loudly than she had anticipated.

"Yes, way," responded Ebony. "We're supposed to be growing and they would definitely help us grow."

"This is going to be a bad idea," Shar kept repeating, even after they made their way over to Marcus, Chase, and Terrence. In fact, it was less of a going over to the boys than a meeting in the middle.

"I guess we both had the same idea," said Terrence, giving Akiya a quick smile, followed by extending his closed hand for a fist bump.

"Wait, wait, wait," interrupted Ebony before the bumping of the fist could commence. "We have to make sure we have some ground rules in place before making any sort of pact."

"Fine," answered Chase, smiling. "I think the first thing we should do is exchange the feedback we got on our last projects. I mean we're hard workers and I don't want to join a team of slackers."

Shar had now stopped chanting, "No way," and jolted up with a look of indignation. "Slackers? We never slack!"

"Well, neither do we," answered Marcus. "So, we just might make a good team. Let's see your feedback." He handed Shar their returned paper.

"I have to admit, you boys did do a great job," answered Ebony as the three girls looked over the boys' paper. "Just some small editing errors, but overall it was good."

"Well, that was probably a bit of all of our faults. I tried to encourage Marcus and Chase to use my speech-to-text software and they had so much fun playing with it, we sort of forgot to actually use it to help edit. So, I guess we can sort of blame my dyslexia for that in a roundabout way," said Terrence, blushing a bit.

"I keep forgetting you're dyslexic too," said Akiya. She was so used to working with Ebony, who was also dyslexic, it was second nature. She immediately felt bad about bringing up the spelling errors.

"No problem, I don't mind. Dyslexia isn't a bad thing, but it does sometimes cause me to not see a spelling mistake here or there. I also use audiobooks instead of regular textbooks. I still do the same work, just in a different way. But that probably means I'm not the best person to do the final edit of the paper." Terrence was smiling now.

"Yeah, we sort of forgot about that part." Marcus smiled. "You three did a great job with your paper—nice research."

Shar responded, more gently this time, "Yes, the research was good. But it was a little boring. Hopefully we can have a little more fun with it this time."

"You came to the right place," answered Marcus and Chase simultaneously.

Chapter Three

"So, where do you start?" Ebony was pulling up a chair and staring intently at the others.

"This seems like it would take a lot of research!" Shar was examining the instructions Mrs. Worthington had placed on the board.

"How hard can it be?" Marcus was looking around the table. "I mean we have an advantage, everyone in our group is a Black American. We can just start with things we know."

"Well, when it comes to the contributions of Black people, I think we should start with our invention of basketball," chimed in Chase. "That's probably why I am so naturally good at it."

"First, what makes you think a Black American invented basketball? Second, do you not remember missing that shot in the cafeteria?" Akiya was trying not to burst into laughter as she grabbed her tablet.

Terrence was already looking information up on his tablet. "Well, Chase, sorry to disappoint you. Basketball wasn't even invented by an American. It was invented by James Naismith, who was born and raised in Canada."

"Well, technically he was in the United States when he invented the game. But here's his picture and I think we can be sure that he wasn't a Black American." Ebony handed her tablet to Chase, who stared at the screen in disbelief.

"Okay, I stand corrected. Cancel my plans of making a sports app with basketball facts about its Black American inventor." He was disappointed but still smiling as he handed the tablet back to Ebony.

"Well, you're already busy with my app anyway, how is it coming along?" Ebony was now looking at Chase in anticipation.

"It's getting closer. We still need to figure out the cloud coverage parameters we're going to be dealing with and the telescope lens we're basing our calculations on," answered Chase without hesitation. He loved talking app design and felt proud that his friends called on his services. He would dive deeply into any topic in order to get his apps just right. Everyone said he could be making a lot of money designing apps and games, but he really did it for the love of coding.

"What in the world are you two talking about?" asked Marcus in surprise. "I didn't know you were designing an app for Ebony."

"With, not for," corrected Ebony. "Chase and I are developing an app to help determine if it makes sense to pull out my telescopes at night. We're figuring out how much is too much cloud cover and when are the best windows for better viewing on any given night."

Terrence gave Chase a high five. "That's a brilliant idea." He turned and gave Ebony a high five as well.

"Chase is helping me with an app as well," said Shar with a smile. "We're designing an app that gives you a list of substitutions if you're trying to make a recipe but you have an allergy to one of the ingredients." She looked down at the table after she spoke. Chase thought he had a clue about why Shar went quiet. He could imagine that she was recounting the situation she told them about, the close call her little brother had last Thanksgiving when someone accidently included pecans in the sweet potato pie they had brought over, thinking that since Joshua was allergic to walnuts, pecans would be an appropriate substitution. They had unfortunately marked the dish as safe at the family potluck since they'd told Shar's mother they had taken into account Joshua's allergies. It was a long and suspenseful two weeks for everyone after that one small bite of pie.

Marcus, always an expert a feeling the tension quickly broke the silence. "Well, unless you are also making an app that tells us the contributions of Black

Americans to our everyday lives, we have got to find a way to get started on this."

"Why don't we start with your dad?" asked Terrence. "He's a college professor, maybe he knows a good book."

"We could ask him, but I already know what he's going to say, which will be for us to do our own homework since he finished school an entire lifetime ago." Marcus was using his deepest voice possible to impersonate his father.

"Well, anything will help. We want this to not just be a bunch of random facts but really good and interesting information." Akiya was looking back at her old group's report and pondering the advice they had gotten to think outside the box.

"Fine, let's head over to my house after school today. My dad should be home early, he doesn't have to teach any night classes this semester."

"Cool. And, since he's going to be home, see if he'll bake us some cookies. His chocolate chip cookies are the best!" said Chase as he rubbed his stomach.

"You ask him, he's your uncle." Marcus laughed. Chase and Marcus looked and acted so much alike that people thought they were brothers. But they were actually first cousins, born only four weeks apart. Marcus' mother was the twin sister of Chase's mother. The boys were practically raised as brothers—they even lived in the same neighborhood.

"Let's save the cookie conversation until after the research conversation. I really want us to do this right and getting pointed in the right direction might be a good start," said Shar.

"Well, in the meantime, I think we need a group name." Chase was already getting up to grab a piece of construction paper. "Every group starts with a good name."

"I'm in!" Ebony was smiling, as she loved being creative.

"It has to be something that represents all of us." Terrence was grabbing a pencil to write down ideas.

"Well, our school name is Global Academy, why not something with that?" Shar asked.

"What about Global Academy Scholars?" asked Akiya.

"No can do," said Marcus.

"Why not?" Akiya asked, trying not to appear too frustrated.

"Global Academy Scholars. G.A.S. As in—gas. Like the group that passes gas. Before you know it, people will be calling us the fart patrol," said Marcus.

"No one would get the fart patrol from Global Academy Scholars," said Akiya, no longer trying not to appear frustrated.

"I would totally go there," said Chase, laughing with Marcus.

Marcus chimed in again, "I like where you're going with it though, Akiya. I think it should be about our school. We are the Global Academy, we're a S.T.E.A.M. school as well. How about we think about something with that?"

Ebony stood up and started to pace slightly. "That's way too long, we would have to shorten it. You know what, I like the gas concept."

"You want to be the fart patrol?" asked Terrence, now a little confused.

"No, but what is gas—beyond farting?" Ebony cut off Marcus and Chase before they could mention it again. "The type of gas most people are familiar with is steam. So, we can have steam in our name."

"I love it!" Chase was already jumping up from his chair. "And we're going to be hunting down information, right? So, what if we were the STEAM Chasers?"

"You really put your own name in there, Chase?" Ebony was smirking and half rolling her eyes.

"No. Well, actually yes. I put all of our names in there. At least a part of everyone's name." Chase was looking at the others triumphantly.

Terrence was writing something on a piece of paper. "Wow! He did put all of our names in there!" He pushed the paper to the center of the table so everyone could see.

S = Shar

T = Terrence

E = Ebony

A = Akiya

M = Marcus

Marcus patted Chase on the back. “You, my man, have the mind of a computer. How did you come up with that so fast?”

“You know me, I love a challenge!” Chase was now standing to take a bow.

“Perfect!” said Shar.

“STEAM Chasers it is,” said Akiya. “And we can start chasing now, it’s time to go.”

The group grabbed their backpacks and headed out the door. By the time everyone had checked in with their parents and headed to Marcus’ house, it was almost four o’clock.

Marcus’ dad met them at the door.

“Hello, Mr. Sparks,” said Ebony.

“Hey, Uncle,” said Chase.

“Before you even ask, no cookies.” Mr. Sparks laughed, grabbing his nephew by the shoulder and giving him a hug. “To what do I owe the pleasure of all of you fine visitors?”

“We need help with an assignment, Dad,” said Marcus.

“Son, I graduated a long time ago. You should be doing your own homework.”

Everyone started to laugh, especially realizing how well Marcus was able to mimic his father’s tone.

“But, Dad, this is right up your alley, it’s all about Black history,” said Marcus, trying to sound convincing.

“Well, not just history,” added Terrence. “We’re supposed to be finding the ways Black Americans have contributed to society.”

“And, considering we didn’t invent basketball, we have a lot of catching up to do,” added Chase with a smile.

“Why would you think we invented basketball?” asked Mr. Sparks.

“Because I am so good at it.” Chase smiled.

“Did you forget what happened in the cafeteria?” asked Shar as she shook her head.

“We really need to make a vow not to speak of that again. I mean, the STEAM Chasers have got to be a united front,” said Chase.

“STEAM Chasers, huh? I like the sound of that. Tell me some more about this project. I won’t do your homework, but I might have some ideas,” said Mr. Sparks. They told him about the assignment and how they wanted their presentation to be fun.

“Well, I have been talking with some of the faculty in our Engineering and Education departments on campus about some ideas for helping students learn more about just this very topic. This might be a good way to test some of those out. But I have to run things by your parents. I’ll text them this evening and have Marcus let you know if it’s a go.”

“Wait, are you going to make us test subjects?” asked Marcus.

"Look, you want me to help you with your homework, you all can help me with mine." Mr. Sparks laughed.

Chapter Four

"My dad gave us the go! He wants us to meet at my house after school today. The only thing he would tell me was to make sure everyone had on good walking shoes." Marcus bounded into the room, letting the words spill out before he even managed to take his seat.

"Great news!" Ebony said. "I was getting worried. I really want to get started. I tried to do a bit of research online, but I wasn't really sure what perspective to take. Should we do athletes, entertainers, politicians? There were so many choices."

"I was hoping we could do something unique, maybe look at people no one talks about very much."

Terrence plopped down on a bean bag chair as he spoke. “I just know I don’t want to present the same type of information as everyone else in the class.”

“I figured that,” answered Marcus. “I told my dad all those things. He said he had some ideas and everyone’s parents were going to be helping to get things together. I guess we have to wait until this afternoon to find out just what this adventure is going to be about.”

Chase stood up and straightened his tie, part of a new clothing trend he was trying to start at the school, although so far, no one had joined him in the cause of wearing ties with jeans and tee-shirts. “I’m just going to need my uncle to step up his game and make sure to have some cookies this time. He cannot expect adventure on an empty stomach!”

“Chase, you do realize that tie would stay put if you actually wore a collared shirt, right?” Akiya, who did have a fashion style everyone tried to copy, was trying to help Chase with his tie as she spoke.

The day seemed to drag by, even though they covered interesting material in class. It was finally time to head out to Marcus' house. They were all talking about the various things that had happened at school that day as the six made their way through Marcus' front door.

"Dad, we're here!" Marcus yelled as he walked into the kitchen. He threw a nod toward Chase and pointed to a plate of chocolate chip and oatmeal cookies.

"You do love me, Uncle!" Chase was already pulling up a cookie as he spoke.

Mr. Sparks walked into the room wearing his usual jeans, button shirt, blazer, and bowtie. "Don't go too hard on those cookies, Chase. Those are for everyone. So, you kids ready to get started?"

Everyone nodded their heads and followed Mr. Sparks into the living room.

"Okay, this is an interactive learning experience that has been set up for you all. Lots of people worked hard on this, including many of your parents. You are going to go to the locations in this folder. There is a clue to lead you to each designated spot. You will know you are in the right spot when you find a yellow envelope. In the envelope will be a hint to whether one of the three items in that space was invented by a Black American or a Black American contributed to that invention. Once you figure out the first item, you will need to figure out the other two items on your own. You should write down the item, the inventor, and the patent number of the invention or improvement. This should give you a good start on your project, but you all will be finishing the rest. You are entitled to one phone call for a hint, so don't waste it." Mr. Sparks was smiling, obviously overjoyed at the challenge he'd helped to create.

"So, when do we start?" asked Shar.

"You start right now," said Mr. Sparks, handing Ebony a yellow folder.

Ebony opened the folder and began reading the first clue.

The first stop that you make, you have been here before.

You know this place well, just open the door.

Three things you will find, this may blow your mind.

You use them quite often; in fact, all the time.

"So, where have we all been before?" asked Chase.

"Well, here, but I don't think that's where we're starting," Marcus answered, looking around the room trying to see if anything about it seemed new.

Akiya stood up. "Where is a place that we go to all the time?"

Terrence jumped up, startling Marcus' cat that dashed under the couch to get away from the commotion. "I've got it! School!"

"Yes! Brilliant!" Marcus was leading the pack out the door.

They made it back to the school quicker than they ever had before.

"Now where do we go?" asked Shar.

"It said to just open the door, I think we would go to Mrs. Worthington's class." Chase was already heading down the hall to the classroom. He passed several classrooms along the way with students engaged in various after school activities. It seemed Global Academy was never closed and always had something interesting going on. He and the rest of the group, who had caught up to him now, may have been tempted to stop and watch students practicing for an upcoming play if they weren't already on a mission. They got to the classroom and Ebony opened the door.

"Well, hello there," said Mrs. Worthington. "I thought I would be seeing you all. Have a look around, just pull the door closed when you're finished." With that, she left the room.

"Okay, we're here, now what?" Terrence was turning in a circle as he surveyed the room. "I have no idea where to start."

"My dad said there would be a yellow envelope, let's try looking for that," said Marcus, who was already looking behind books on a bookcase at the front of the classroom.

Akiya responded, "Why don't we try to see if something has been added to the room? That might be a good clue."

Chase stood next to her. "That's a great idea. The room looks pretty similar to how it was when we left. Except that." Chase was pointing to a folding chair that was sitting next to Mrs. Worthington's desk.

Shar walked to the back of the chair and squawked with delight, "I found it!" Sure enough, she was taking off a yellow envelope that had been attached to the back of the chair.

Congratulations, my little friends

It seems your adventure now begins

Who made me? And then look more,

Two additional things you are searching for.

Chase had his phone out, searching for the inventor of the folding chair. "Nathanial Alexander invented the collapsing folding chair. He was awarded patent #997,108 on July 4th, 1911."

"Wow," said Marcus. "The folding chair. We made that?"

"So, what exactly is a patent?" asked Chase to no one in particular.

Akiya was ready with an answer, as usual. "A patent basically identifies the person as the owner of that invention. You can keep other people from making it without your permission."

"Oh, so you mean there is a way for me to protect all the awesome inventions in my head, like the weaponized puppy army?" asked Marcus, who was not cracking a smile.

"Puppy army?" asked Shar. "Are you serious? What are you going to do to defenseless little puppies?"

"Not real puppies! What do you think I am, some sort of monster? Mechanical puppies!"

Chase chimed in, "Oh, now that sounds awesome!"

"Of course," answered Marcus. "They're going to fight crime. I was thinking of equipping each of them with a special type of laser."

Now Chase was really intrigued. “Like laser eyes?”

“No way, too cliché. Even Superman has laser eyes.

Terrence was also now drawn into the conversation. “So, the mouth?”

“Nope. These aren’t dragons, they’re puppies. I figure they should act like puppies do. So, I think the lasers should come out of the butt. Bad guys wouldn’t even see it coming.”

Ebony was shaking her head. “Marcus, sometimes I wonder about what rolls around in that head of yours. Laser puppy derrieres?”

“Have you ever smelled dog farts? They’re already pretty toxic. Just amp that up a bit more and condense it into some sort of solid that we could have come out with a controlled photon blast and those puppies are fighting crime like true heroes.”

Chase was ready to get started right away. “I wonder if we could bottle the smell to begin testing. Terrence, can we hook something up to your dog to collect dog fart smell?”

Terrence was quite aware of how Marcus and Chase's projects sometimes went. "Umm, I'm not sure about that."

Marcus decided to jump in with trying to persuade him. "Terrence, how often do we let people in on our projects? This could make millions. Plus, it's totally legal!"

"Flatulence-based photon lasers are legal? I'm going with a no on that," chimed in Shar.

"Shar, don't be a hater!" retorted Marcus.

Ebony spoke up. "I think she is being a realist, not a hater."

Chase put his arm around Terrence's shoulder. "Ignore them, Terrence. We could be saving the world. Bottling dog farts has to be good for the environment. We will even use recycled metal for the puppies. Shar, you know all about chemistry. Can a gas become a solid?"

Shar was immediately conflicted. She didn't want to support the boys in their crazy scheme, but she just couldn't let a chemistry question pass her by.

"Well?" prodded Marcus.

"Yes. In some instances a gas can become a solid. Kind of like dry ice, which is really dangerous when not handled properly."

"See, we could totally do this!" Marcus and Chase were giving each other a high five.

"Did you two not hear the dangerous part?" asked Shar, wondering if encouraging the two at all was a good idea.

Akiya knew this could go on forever, so she tried to get everyone back on track. "Okay, no more puppy army talk. Now we have to figure out two other things in this room that were invented by Black Americans. "

"Hey, did one of you put this on my shelf?" Ebony was holding a sharpener. Everyone shook their head no. "Well, I know it isn't mine. Let's look it up and see what we find."

Akiya had her tablet out. "What am I looking for, just pencil sharpener?"

"No, I think it has to be something more than just that. There's already a pencil sharpener on the wall and

Mrs. Worthington has an electric pencil sharpener on her desk," answered Shar.

"Oh my gosh, this is awesome." Akiya almost sang the words. "The Love Sharpener. It's a portable pencil sharpener that actually looks similar to the one you're holding. The inventor was John Lee Love."

"Well, he wins with the best last name ever," said Chase, straightening his tie again.

"I guess naming a pencil sharpener after himself means you two probably had a lot of things in common." Shar laughed. "He was awarded patent #594,114 on November 23, 1897."

"This is so cool. I mean—a version of the pencil sharpener. We actually made that." Marcus was once again shaking his head in amazement and now holding the pencil sharpener in his hand.

"Okay, just one more item to find!" said Terrence. Everyone spread out over the room, looking to see what they might find that was a little bit out of place or hadn't been noticed before.

Shar then noticed something she hadn't before, a book sitting on a window sill. She may not have noticed it but for one detail—it was standing upright and had a bow wrapped around it. "Hey, has anyone seen that book before?" she asked the group.

"No, I walked right past it and didn't even notice," answered Terrence, heading toward the window.

"Wait, we aren't really saying that Black Americans invented books, are we? I mean, we have done a lot of things, but I am pretty sure writing has been around for a lot longer than America." Chase spoke as he joined the group gathered around the book.

"*Clotel*; or, *The President's Daughter*," read Akiya slowly. "Has anyone heard of this book? I know I never heard of it before."

"A book you haven't read? I didn't think that was possible!" Marcus was only halfway joking as Akiya was one of the most prolific readers he knew.

"Who wrote it?" asked Ebony.

"William Wells Brown," answered Terrence. "Can you look him up, please?"

It didn't take Ebony long to find the answer. "Wow, this is amazing!" she squealed.

"What?" asked Chase, hardly able to contain his enthusiasm.

"It says that William Wells Brown is considered the first Black American to publish a full fictional novel. He published this book in London in 1853. He was an escaped slave who moved to London and didn't want to come back to America for fear of being recaptured and sent back to a plantation due to the 1850 Fugitive Slave Act. This book is a fictional account of a girl named Clotel and her sister, who were supposed to be slave daughters of Thomas Jefferson. Wow, what a brave man to write this kind of book, especially at that time in history."

"So, he didn't invent writing, but he definitely started the genre of Black American writers. I knew I'd heard of the poems of Philis Wheatly being published in the late 1700's, but I never thought about who might've been the first Black American to publish a novel. Now we know," said Marcus, smiling brightly while looking at the book.

"I thought we were looking for patents. Books don't have patents do they?" Shar was writing information down in her notebook when she asked the question.

Akiya responded, "Books don't have patents, but they do have copyrights. Copyrights are similar in a lot of ways to patents. For instance, patents protect inventions and ideas, while copyrights protect intellectual property."

"Wait, you mean we have to get a copyright for our brain? And, if we don't have a copyright—does that mean we haven't had intellectual thoughts?" Terrence was looking with suspicion at Akiya.

"Not intellectual thoughts, Terrence, intellectual property. For instance, people get copyrights for novels, movies, poetry, songs, even computer software and architectural drawings. So, his novel being copywritten starts the trend of the intellectual property of Black Americans being protected. Because he was free by escaping to Europe, he was able to own his own words and ushered in many free writers, such a Fredrick Douglass who published books here in the United States."

Ebony chimed in to the discussion as she looked up from her tablet, "This is so interesting. Most of the earliest Black American writers were in fact slaves when their work was written. In fact, most of them were women. A lot of people have heard of the works of Phillis Wheatley, but it says here the earliest known writing of a Black American was Lucy Terry, who wrote a piece called, "*Bar Fights*" in 1746. She was a slave, so unfortunately wasn't given control of her own writings, some weren't actually published until the 1850's, long after she had died. Jupiter Hammon published a book of poems in America in 1761, but he was also a slave at the time, so wasn't given full control over his own writing. But, with the publication of Clotel by William Wells Brown, Black Americans were finally able to write about the things they wanted and could actually be given the protection of their intellectual property. Mr. Brown showed this by writing on such a controversial topic of the children Thomas Jefferson fathered with the woman he kept in slavery, Sally Hemings. Even though this book was fiction, he wrote it and published it and even traveled all over Europe giving lectures about the book! He couldn't come back to the United States due to the Fugitive Slave Act, which would have meant he could have been taken back into slavery."

"And I can't wait to read this book!" Akiya was already walking toward the book sign-out sheet as she spoke.

"Let me know as soon as you're finished, I want to read it next." Ebony was quickly writing her name down in the reserve column of the sign-out sheet.

Shar walked over to her. "I thought you were on your mythology kick? Are you leaving mythology behind for now?"

"No way. I love mythology and there are never things to run out of reading. Plus, Greek and Roman mythology are pretty important when researching astronomy."

"Really, how so?" Terrence was now walking over, intrigued by the conversation.

"The names of planets and moons in our solar system are heavily influenced by Greek and Roman mythology. It helps to memorize them if you know the myths well."

Akiya chimed in, "And I bet it really helps with our Level-Up Language Challenge!"

"What's the Level-Up Language Challenge?" asked Terrence, now really excited the six of them would be working together.

"We each keep a running list of new and interesting words we encounter. We then try to really learn them and start to incorporate them as much as possible. It makes reading a lot easier and it has helped a ton in classes like science and literature."

"I think I am already doing something a little bit similar. Since I have dyslexia, it tends to be easier to read with what they call context clues—so understanding what the story is about. The more important context clues I know, the easier it is for me to read a little bit faster. I wonder if writing down the words like you all would help with my spelling a little bit as well."

"I guess we're all kind of doing this a bit. Marcus and I just do it in a fun way. We play all these word games with our parents and we got tired of losing. So, we went into the Boulderdash game box and took out all the word cards and looked them up. Now we hardly ever lose!"

Shar gasped, "Chase, that's cheating!"

"No Shar, that is habituating to a higher level language to rule game night." Marcus and Chase gave each other a high five. "And now we can join the Level-up Language Challenge."

"Okay, now back to the subject at hand, did we complete our list?" Akiya was going back to the folder.

"We did it! We found the three items in this classroom. Let's look at the next clue then send a text to our parents letting them know where we think we're heading next," said Terrence, opening the yellow folder for the next clue.

"I have to admit this is turning into a really amazing adventure. Best homework assignment of the year!" said Marcus as he gave Chase a high five.

Chapter Five

The group formed a circle around Terrence as he read the next clue aloud.

Wonderful, team, you are on a roll
But there is more that must unfold
As you check in with my little sis
Keep your eyes open or you might miss
How you get where you have to be
Would have been much harder and slower without me

"Well, we definitely know where we're going," said Chase, grabbing his backpack.

"What do you mean?" asked Ebony as she grabbed her tote and purse.

"My mom is Mrs. Sparks' little sister," answered Chase matter-of-factly.

"Wait, I thought they were twins," said Terrence.

"They are," chimed in Marcus. "But, even with twins, someone had to come first. My mom was born two minutes earlier than Chase's mom, so he always calls her little sister to bug her."

"So, we need to go to your house?" asked Akiya, pulling on her infinity scarf that complemented her outfit perfectly.

"No," said Chase as he turned the door handle. "My mom isn't at the house right now, she's at her office."

"I love going to visit! She is on the eighth floor and the view is amazing!" said Marcus.

"Well, we have to keep our eyes peeled on the way. The clue says the next thing is how we get to the office," said Terrence.

"Well, the way we're getting there is walking. Her office is just four blocks away at the Oxland Building," answered Chase.

They talked feverishly as they walked as quickly as they could. They looked around a lot as they made their way to the office, but nothing seemed to jump out at them, even as they made their way up to the big glass doors that read in bright turquoise letters, "Oxland."

"Do you think it has something to do with the door to the building?" asked Marcus as he grabbed the handle.

"No yellow envelopes yet—let's keep looking as we walk," Shar spoke in her quiet, grown-up voice as they entered the building. She had a great way of blending in with adults when they were off school grounds. She had a way of asserting herself that caused even her elders to speak to her as an equal rather than a kid.

They tried to look inconspicuous as they peered into the backs of chairs, into flowerpots, and even into trashcans making their way to the elevator. As they approached the elevator, a tall man wearing an expensive looking suit appeared around the corner. "Chase! How are you doing? Here to see your mom?"

"Yes, Mr. Highlander."

"I see you brought some friends with you," said Mr. Highlander as he reached out his hand to the others.

"Yes, sir. These are my classmates Akiya, Ebony, Shar, Terrence, and you know Marcus," answered Chase, trying to sound mature. "We're working on a school project and needed to check in with my mom."

"Absolutely." Mr. Highlander smiled. "I am sure your mom will be a big help, whatever the project is. She is the top real estate agent in the firm, so if you all need to buy some property she would definitely be the one to ask."

"Thanks, Mr. Highlander. No real estate deals for this project, but we might be doing some walking around town. We're on a bit of an adventure," said Marcus with a wink.

"Well, the town is yours to explore and I am sure whatever you need you will find. I absolutely love that school of yours, your mom tells me so many great things about it. I wish it were available when my kids were in middle school. Heck, I wish it were there when I was in middle school. But the dinosaurs still roaming around probably would have knocked it down." His joke caused him to roar with laughter.

"Well, it isn't every day we meet a million-year-old." Akiya laughed. "And here I wouldn't have pegged you a day over forty."

"You're hired for whatever pay you want to start," said Mr. Highlander. "You are a brilliant young lady. But I won't hold you all up any longer. Have fun meeting up with your mom, and don't let her do all the work for you on your project."

"We won't," the group answered in unison.

They got on the elevator as it arrived, having a lively discussion about what their city may have looked like fifty years ago, let alone a million years ago. Even as they got off on the eighth floor, they were still completely engrossed in their conversation. As they walked to the end of the hall, Chase spoke up. "Here's my mom's office." They entered the office and were greeted by a beautiful woman who looked strikingly similar to Chase.

"Oh, you all made it! How did the first part of the hunt go?" Mrs. Thornton asked while she gave each person a big hug.

"Hey, Auntie," said Marcus in the most Kilmonger voice he could muster. He thought the best part of having an aunt was being able to use that line from his favorite movie.

"It's gone well, although we have no idea what we're supposed to be looking for in your office," said Chase, starting to look around for an envelope.

"It isn't in here, Chase. You mean to tell me you guys missed your clue?" asked Mrs. Thornton.

"Was it Mr. Highlander? Because we talked to him for a while, but he didn't give us an envelope," said Ebony, looking perplexed.

"Nope, not Mr. Highlander. Although it is interesting that he was sneaking out early." Mrs. Thornton laughed. Why don't you all retrace your steps and rethink about the clue? I'll be here waiting."

They funneled back out of the office and made their way back to the elevator. "We looked everywhere in the lobby. I'm not sure how we could have missed it. Maybe it was in the bathroom," said Marcus, rubbing his head as he re-read the clue.

The elevator doors opened and everyone piled inside for another ride. As the doors closed, a yellow envelope was attached to one of the door panels.

"How did we miss this?" screamed Shar. She grabbed the envelope off the door. They felt silly as they got to the first floor, only to immediately ride back up to the eighth.

They went back into Mrs. Thornton's office with the envelope in their hands. "Ah, I see you found it this time," she said with a laugh.

"So, a Black American invented the elevator?" asked Shar hesitantly.

“Not quite, Shar,” said Mrs. Thornton. “Where did you get the envelope from exactly?”

“The elevator doors!” said Terrence, almost to himself.

Akiya was already on her tablet and reading aloud, “Mr. Alexander Miles received patent 371,207 on October 11, 1887. He invented a mechanism to open and close doors automatically. This invention greatly improved elevator safety.”

Marcus was looking intently over Akiya’s shoulder. “Wow, we made that?”

“Yes, Marcus,” said Mrs. Thornton, smiling and giving him a big hug. “We made that. Just think of how many lives that were saved when elevator doors could open and close only at safe points and safe times. It was a wonderful and innovative improvement. Now, here is your next clue.”

“Thanks so much!” exclaimed Ebony as she grabbed the letter.

She read loudly so that everyone could hear.

Congratulations on a job well done
However, your adventure has just begun
Now go to that grand square where metal and light
Lets you know when you have permission to go left or right
Another hint for the next place
Each of the things you will find help keep you safe

"What could metal and light be asking about?" Terrence wondered as he closed the folder.

"It talks about the metal and light letting you know if you can go left or right. When do we ask something if we can go left or right?" Shar was sitting in a chair with her legs crossed and her hands on her head.

"Maybe it isn't specific left or right but about directions in general. Oh, I know—think about the grand square part. Where is the grand square around here?" Marcus was standing up triumphantly and walking toward the door.

"Not quite sure what he's talking about, but I think we should follow him," said Akiya as she grabbed her backpack and headed out the door, following Marcus.

"Well, I guess you all are on your way to the next clue!" said Mrs. Thornton with a huge smile.

"I think Marcus knows—the rest of us don't have a clue," answered Terrence.

Mrs. Thornton gave Chase a big hug. "Well, go follow your cousin, he seems to be on to something. And call if you need anything!"

Everyone said a quick goodbye to Mrs. Thornton and ran toward the elevator to catch up with Marcus and Akiya. Marcus didn't say anything, but the smile indicated he had a big idea about where, if not what, the next clue was.

"Marcus, where are you taking us?" asked Shar, saying out loud what everyone else was thinking.

"I think I know what we're looking for. Well, sort of. It can be one of two things, either a crosswalk or a traffic light. Let's check the crosswalk first." They rushed out of the elevator as soon as the doors opened.

"Thanks for the safe exit, Mr. Miles!" Ebony was waving at the elevator doors as they made it to the lobby. A few adults looked into the elevator to try to see whom Ebony might be talking to, but there was no time to stop and explain. Marcus was walking fast and everyone was trying to keep up.

They got to the crosswalk, two blocks from the Oxland Building. "Okay, this corner has the most signs and the safest signs to look around. I figure it must be something to do with giving us directions. So, maybe we should start looking around poles. The group started to walk toward one pole that looked like it had a piece of paper attached to it. "This is just a sign about a garage sale this weekend, no yellow envelope." Terrence looked disappointed as he pointed to the bright orange sign attached to the crosswalk.

"You don't think someone accidentally took down our envelope when they were attaching their sign, do you? Maybe we should look in the grass over there as well, just in case it got blown away from the crosswalk," said Shar as she walked to an area with grass that didn't seem like it had been cut in a week or two. Terrence, Marcus and Ebony followed her. Akiya and Chase looked in another patch of grass. While they were looking, they also took the time to talk about what they had learned so far as well as speculate on what they might find during the rest of their hunt.

They had been looking, talking, and laughing for around fifteen minutes when Terrence spoke up. "Okay, I don't think our letter is in this grass. And this is a four way stop and I don't see anything yellow on any of those signs from here. Maybe we should head down to the traffic light crosswalk. The pole is bigger and it covers a little more of the riddle as well."

Ebony chimed in, "Yeah, the traffic light would definitely fit into the riddle more, let's go, everyone!"

As they grabbed their bags and headed for the traffic light, they heard a siren.

Chapter Six

As they grabbed their bags and headed down the short block to the traffic light, the siren got louder. “Oh man, I don’t want to get in the way of police business, maybe we should take a break until it passes,” said Akiya. As she spoke, a police car came into view. The police officer appeared to look at them quickly as he passed. He got to the corner and made a U-turn.

“Whoa, are we in the middle of a bank heist or something like that? I don’t even want to be close enough to see a police chase, let’s go back to your mom’s office until the police finish.” Terrence had stopped to turn around.

Chase spoke quickly. “Terrence, don’t move. Nobody move.”

The police car was now stopped at the corner they had just come from. The group was now halfway between the crosswalk they left and the light they were headed toward.

“Chase, what are you talking about? We don’t need to be in the way of police work. I mean this is fun and all, but I don’t think our parents want us between the police and some bank robber or murderer. I mean really, what if they’re chasing a murderer? We need to get out of here,” said Akiya as she started to walk.

Chase spoke again. “Akiya, don’t move. Please, don’t move. That cop isn’t chasing a bank robber or a murderer—that cop is looking for us.”

Marcus looked at Chase in amazement. “Thunder, are you serious? What makes you think that cop is looking for us? He has his lights on, he’s going to the scene of some crime or helping some cat stuck in a tree.”

Shar said softly, “Fire fighters help cats in trees. Police officers fight crime. We need to get out of the way and leave.”

“Listen, everyone, just stop moving. Don’t grab your bag, don’t reach into your pocket. Don’t do anything but stand still.” Chase was barely moving as he spoke.

They watched the police officer get out of his car. As he closed his door, they saw him speak into the radio that was attached to his shoulder. Another police car was pulling in behind him. The two officers spoke briefly. The second officer then headed to the grassy area the group had been in searching for the envelope. “Do they think we did something?” asked Marcus with just a hint of frustration in his voice.

“Just breathe, Marcus; we’re good. Just like we were taught,” said Chase gently.

“What, do you guys get stopped by the police a lot? What the heck is going on, Chase and Marcus?” asked Akiya, who was now visibly shaking.

"No, we've never been questioned by the police. Our parents just gave us 'the talk.' I promise to tell you all about it later, but for right now, just follow our lead. And please, don't move," said Chase, seeming more mature than they had ever seen him before.

"Hey, kids, can you guys tell me what you have been up to around here?" asked the officer. They couldn't make out the expression on his face. It wasn't anger, but he also wasn't smiling.

Chase spoke first. "Hello, Officer. My name is Chase Thornton, and I am eleven years old. My mother is at work in the Oxland Building. You can call my mother if you would like." Marcus then spoke. "Hello, Officer. My name is Marcus Sparks, and I am eleven years old. My father is Doctor Sparks, a professor at the University. He's at home right now, and I would like to call him if that's okay."

The second officer approached quickly. "I couldn't find anything, so they must still have it on them." She didn't look at the group as she spoke.

"Have what on us?" asked Ebony. "What are you talking about? We didn't have anything."

"Please don't say anything else, Ebony." Marcus was speaking to Ebony but looking at the officers.

"Officer, we are all only eleven years old. Is it okay if we call one of our parents?" asked Chase calmly. At that moment, they saw Mr. Highlander passing in his car. He stopped at the opposite curb and called out, "Chase, are you guys okay?"

The female officer answered, "We got a call from a concerned citizen, sir. We are just asking them what they were doing."

Mr. Highlander spoke calmly, but loudly. "The kids were not committing any crimes, they were just in the building. I know these kids, I'm sure they weren't doing anything wrong."

The officer responded quickly, "Let us do our job and if they haven't done anything wrong, we will let them go."

Mr. Highlander looked angry but started driving again.

"He left us. He left us." Akiya started to cry and kept repeating, "He left us."

Chase moved closer to her. "We'll be fine, we didn't do anything wrong."

The first officer started speaking. "Hey. kids, I'm Officer Mitchell. We got a call about some possible trouble and we just stopped to talk." The group could tell he was forcing himself to sound friendly.

Suddenly, they heard someone yell, "I'm filming all of this. Why are you all messing with these kids? I'm getting it all on camera and it is going to the cloud." It was a young woman who looked like she might be a college student. She was standing defiantly and holding up her camera.

The female officer approached her. "We don't need anyone causing trouble, ma'am."

"Oh, I'm not causing any trouble. Just filming live for the whole world to see what's being done to these kids. Please, continue!"

Chase and Marcus looked at each other. They were prepared for how to handle a stop, they weren't prepared for how to handle a stop that was live streaming to the world. Now they really wished they could have called one of their parents.

Officer Mitchell said quickly, "Officer Carpenter, it's fine. This may all have been a misunderstanding. Let's just hear from the kids."

Officer Carpenter looked unhappy but didn't approach the woman filming.

Officer Mitchell looked back at the group. "Can you all tell me what you were doing over in the grassy area?"

Marcus cleared his throat nervously. "Officer Mitchell, we will gladly tell you everything, but I really would like permission to call my dad so that he can come as well. He would want to be here."

"Answer the questions first," Officer Carpenter responded in a not-so-kind voice.

"Officer Carpenter, I think it will be no problem for him to call his dad," said Officer Mitchell.

"Thank you so much, Officer Mitchell. I'll call my dad, Doctor Sparks. May I get my phone out of my back pocket?" Marcus paused, not moving until Officer Mitchell spoke.

"Of course you can call your father—I think it would be best."

Marcus called his father and asked him to come meet them at the corner. He spoke calmly and clearly telling his dad exactly where to come and that the police were there as well.

Akiya continued to cry and she was now holding Chase's hand.

Terrence hadn't said much during the encounter, but Ebony could tell that something was wrong. "Terrence, are you okay?" she asked softly. Terrence didn't answer right away, he tried to shake his head yes, but seemed to be struggling even with the slightest movement. He then grabbed his stomach and stepped to the edge of the sidewalk. He took one step into the grass and then vomited.

Officer Carpenter approached Terrence and put her hand on his shoulder. "Are you okay, young man? Do you need something?" Terrence shook his head then dropped to his knees and started to cry. “It’s okay, you’re not in trouble. We just wanted to see what you all were up to. We got a call that there was a possible crime taking place, that some people were possibly selling drugs and we had to investigate.” All of the frustration that was once in Officer Carpenter’s voice had vanished. She no longer looked upset, she looked concerned. There was now sadness in her eyes as she realized just how scared the group must be.

Terrence vomited again and said, “I wanted to run. I almost ran. What would have happened if I ran?”

“What’s going on? Isn’t this enough? You got these kids so scared they’re sick!” yelled the woman who continued to film. Officer Mitchell looked up at the woman filming but said nothing.

Officer Carpenter continued to hold her hand on Terrence’s shoulder and asked softly and more gently than they had heard her speak before, “Why would you have run?”

Terrence answered, his hand still on his stomach, “We wanted to get out of your way. We thought you were chasing bad guys and we wanted to make sure we didn't interfere. We thought you were chasing a bank robber or a murderer, not some kids out doing their homework. Would you really have thought we were the bad guys because we ran?"

Officer Carpenter looked up at Officer Mitchell and then looked to Terrence. "I think I would have and I am sorry. We were really trying to find out what was going on, but our caller said some people were selling drugs here. Our number one priority is keeping drugs out of our community."

"Why would someone say we were selling drugs? We didn't even do anything. We came out of the Oxland Building and came straight to the crosswalk. We looked around the poles and when we didn't see our envelope we thought maybe someone accidentally knocked it down, so we were looking to see if it blew in the grass," answered Shar, looking shocked at the thought of being considered a criminal.

"What do you mean you were doing your homework?" asked Officer Mitchell. "What sort of envelope were you looking for?"

Marcus spoke up as he placed his phone back into his pocket, "Our parents were helping us with our homework. Our assignment was to find various contributions Black Americans have made to our society that impact our everyday life. We were following the next clue. We thought it might be the crosswalk, but when we didn't see the letter, we went to look around in the grass thinking maybe it had blown off or something. We decided to go look at the pole for the traffic light. That was when we heard the sirens."

Officer Mitchell had a stunned look on his face—then he looked at Officer Carpenter. Officer Mitchell spoke again. "Can we go look at the light together? It isn't that I don't believe you, I do. I would just love to see this for myself." He was smiling.

"Can she come too?" asked Shar, pointing to the woman filming. "She's been making sure we are okay and I think she might want to know what this was all about as well."

"Absolutely," responded Officer Mitchell. "Come on, our camera person, the kids want you to get this on film."

The woman looked startled at first then walked across the street to meet up with the group. They all walked toward the light. Akiya was still shaking and still holding Chase's hand. Officer Carpenter was walking next to Terrence with her hand on his shoulder. Ebony and Shar were telling the woman recording why they were all heading toward the light. Marcus was walking next to Officer Mitchell. As they got closer to the pole with the button for the crosswalk used to change the light when a pedestrian was ready to cross, they saw the bright yellow envelope. "There it is!" shouted Shar.

"I have got to get this on film!" said the woman with the camera.

"Can you grab it down, Marcus?" asked Officer Mitchell. Marcus grabbed the envelope and began to read.

The ingenious addition to the common device
Has saved untold numbers of lives
It provided the simplest but most important fix
By alerting drivers to what would happen next
Reduce your speed even if you are not doing the top
The light is about to change so be prepared to stop

Ebony, who had pulled out her phone, started to read out loud, "Garrett Morgan received patent number 1,475,074 in 1923. It wasn't the first traffic signal, those had been around since 1868. However, it was the first ever signal to include the third position of the yellow warning light, letting crossing vehicles know to prepare to stop. This helped to significantly cut down on the many collisions between cars, buggies, bicycles, and even pedestrians that would share crowded roadways."

"Wow!" exclaimed Marcus with a smile. "We made that!"

"I had no idea," said Officer Mitchell, shaking his head and smiling.

"I can't believe there didn't used to be a warning light," said Officer Carpenter. "Can you imagine how many people were hurt due to lights going from green to red instantly?"

"Chase!" They turned as a voice called it. It was Mrs. Thornton running down the sidewalk followed closely by Mr. Highlander.

"See, Akiya, he didn't leave us. He went to get my mom," said Chase. Akiya had just begun to stop shaking. She ran and collapsed into Mrs. Thornton's arms. She didn't realize she had so many tears left inside her, but as her shoulders shook and the tears ran down her cheeks, she was finally able to admit just how scared she had been. Mr. Sparks was also walking down the street now in the other direction, having parked his car in a nearby parking lot.

"What in the world is going on?" he asked as he came up.

"I have most of it on film," said the lady who had been recording. "I can send you the footage."

"Thank you so much," replied Dr. Sparks. "That would be great. We'll speak with the officers and see how this all came about."

"I can get her information and I'll stay with the kids while you all talk." Mr. Highlander was moving toward the woman who had been filming.

It was only after Officer Carpenter was convinced Terrence was feeling better and would not need medical help that she took her arm off of his shoulder. "You are a great kid, Terrence. I am so sorry we scared you." She spoke softly as she headed off to talk to Mrs. Thornton and Dr. Sparks.

Chapter Seven

Officer Mitchell told Dr. Sparks and Mrs. Thornton about the phone call to the police. Mrs. Thornton gasped, "This is something you see on television, but you don't think it will happen to your own kids."

"The kids were great, they did nothing wrong. In fact, they did everything right. Marcus and Chase in particular knew exactly what to do."

"We had *the talk*,'" replied Mr. Sparks, looking both relieved and frustrated at the same time. "I was hoping it was an unnecessary experience for them. Clearly, it was not."

Officer Carpenter then spoke. "I am so sorry. We were operating under the 911 call indicating some sort of drug deal in progress. We didn't even know they were kids until we showed up. We could have used some Garrett Morgan and proceeded with a bit more caution." Embarrassment showed on her face as her eyes pleaded with everyone as she searched for the right words to say.

"This is a great activity you're doing with the kids. I'm so impressed with it and I am so sorry this extraordinary scavenger hunt was interrupted in this way. Please, don't hesitate to have the kids continue," said Officer Mitchell. "Please let them know they have every right to be in this town, all over this town, doing just this. They did nothing wrong, the phone call was wrong, and we should have proceeded with more caution. Here we thought we were doing pretty well. But clearly we need better procedures—they were so scared of us, and that is not the relationship I want young people to have with police officers."

Mr. Sparks spoke calmly, but his eyes showed frustration. "I am sure we all have something we can learn from this."

"Do you have Terrence's parents' number?" asked Officer Carpenter. "I would like to talk to them. Terrence got very upset. His stomach was tied into such knots he actually vomited."

Mrs. Thornton gave Officer Carpenter the phone number for Terrence's parents. She reached out and patted Terrence on the back. He worked hard to control his breathing. Terrence didn't want his mom to worry. He had worked hard to learn to manage his anxiety and he had been doing great. But what kid wouldn't have an anxiety attack at this? Akiya was having just as difficult a time. Chase and Marcus were trying to look strong, but they had worry on their faces, and Marcus' anger was hard to ignore. Chase quickly noticed that Ebony was looking into space, almost in shock. He remembered she often tried to escape stressful situations by thinking about the cosmos and the vastness of the universe or any place that wasn't here on Earth. She looked like she just might build her own rocket right there on the street to fly away. Chase thought to himself that Shar was the bravest of all because she openly wept. Her strength was in not trying to hide her tears.

Mr. Sparks walked over to the STEAM Chasers and spoke quietly. “I’m sorry. I should have anticipated something like this. We just never expected anyone around here would call the police like that. How about we all go home?”

“No,” Terrence answered quietly but defiantly. “I don’t mean to be rude, Mr. Sparks. But everyone keeps saying we didn’t do anything wrong. Well, if we didn’t do anything wrong, why do we have to go home?”

“He’s right.” Akiya stepped slowly forward, looking quickly to Chase then to Ebony, and gave a soft smile, letting them know she was okay now, braver. “I want to finish my homework. This project is due soon and everyone worked so hard to help us do this. If we belong in our own community, then we should be able to be here and not run home and hide.”

Mrs. Thornton gave her a big hug. “You are absolutely right. You all should absolutely finish your homework. I’ll walk with you if you like.”

"Thanks for the offer, Mom, but we're good." Chase was giving his mother a big hug. Although he did give a fleeting look to Marcus who still seemed to be a bit upset.

Ebony put her arm through Shar's and said, "I'm in if you are!"

Shar laughed and spoke up. "No doubt. We got this!"

Chase and Marcus gave each other a nod and shouted, "STEAM Chasers assemble!" Everyone broke out in laughter.

"STEAM Chasers, I love it!" Officer Mitchell was saying goodbye to Mr. Highlander. "Absolutely perfect. And you all, please give me a call if you have any trouble. I'll keep my eye out to make sure no one bothers you all again. Have fun with the rest of your steam chasing!"

"Next clue?" asked Ebony.

"Right here!" Marcus was holding the envelope with another piece of paper inside.

Look to the left and then to the right
There is something that is common that will be in your sight
It used to take much longer to communicate
If I wanted to tell you something important I had to wait
Until you had time to go where it went
I had to say where it was as well as what I sent
Now over rain, sleet, ice, and snow
I can tell you directly what I need you to know.

Terrence stopped and sat down on the ground. He placed his book bag next to him. The gold stripe down the side glinted in the sunlight along with the Global Academy keychain hanging from the zipper.

"Are you okay? Do you feel sick again?" asked Chase, walking closer to him.

"No, I'm fine. My brain felt like it was moving too fast! I thought if I sat down, I could slow down and think."

"Good idea! The only thing that would make this better is if someone thought to bring a snack." Marcus had sat down next to Terrence. He was looking at Ebony with a small smirk. She rolled her eyes. Everyone knew Ebony always had the best snacks. She was always on the run, so her mom made her keep something to eat in case time got away from her. This time was no exception. There were five pairs of eyes now looking at her in anticipation.

"Okay, fine. I have some granola bars, then we need to get back to the clue!"

"I work so much better on a full stomach!" Chase ate his granola bar in two big bites. Shar took her time, eating in small bites so she could savor the dried fruits that were embedded within the chewy granola. Ebony had even made sure Shar's bar had no nuts just in case her little brother met her at the door before she could wash her hands and brush her teeth once she got home.

Akiya was drinking from her pink water bottle and looking around. "What would communication have to do with weather? Maybe a phone booth?"

“I don’t think there are any phone booths around here,” answered Shar. “Maybe a computer to send email or a cell phone to text messages?”

Terrence was looking around when he zeroed in on a mailbox. It was a big blue one, the kind used to send mail if you were out and didn’t want to go to the post office. On the side was the white emblem with a blue figure and in bright blue letters the words “United States Postal Service.” “Could the clue be talking about regular mail?” Terrence was already on his feet even as he asked the question.

They made their way to the mailbox and looked around. Akiya reached for the handle and pulled down the little door that was heavier than would be expected. On the back of the door was a yellow envelope.

“You guessed it! Philip B. Downing invented the street letter box. This was the precursor to the modern-day mailbox used by people today. He received U.S. Patents 462,092 and 462,093 for his invention in 1891. This blue mailbox was most similar to his metal mailbox invention that also had four legs and a large hinged door," read Akiya

"That is so cool!" Shar was walking around the mailbox and smiling. "The next time I write my granny a letter, I am going to ask her if she knew that a Black American was the person who helped make the way we communicate easier!"

"You still send letters, Shar? You know there is an app for that, right?" Chase was now shaking his head at the mere thought of how inefficient it all seemed.

"Chase, my grandmother just got a cellphone for the first time a couple months ago, and she still doesn't know how to use it. Plus, she has been writing me since I first learned to read. It's our thing and I like it."

"Just make sure not to put any big secrets in the letter. Do you know how easy it would be to intercept?" Marcus chimed in as if he was really concerned.

"Marcus, this is my grandmother—not some undercover secret spy!" Shar was now laughing along with Akiya and Ebony.

"Marcus, what in the world do you talk about with your grandparents?"

Chase jumped in front of Marcus and yelled, "Don't answer! Don't answer! They are not safe. Do you know how easily they can be hacked?"

Terrence was now looking at the two cousins in utter bemusement. "Okay, now I'm concerned about what you two talk about with your grandparents!"

Chase and Marcus just looked at each other and put on their usual Thunder and Lightning grins.

"Well, since they can't release any state secrets, let's read some more. There is something on the back of this letter.

#

You are now off and on your way

The next stop is a place it is now in play

You don't need a bike, bus, or car

You can walk there, it isn't far

No need to waddle or to roam

In fact, one of you calls this place home
When you get to the place that you chose
Head for the flowers and then strike a pose

"Sweet, we go to one of our houses!" Ebony was a bit relieved, still shaken up by the police encounter but wanting to seem brave for her friends.

"Okay, who lives the closest to where we are now?" Marcus was looking around at the group.

Terrence was the first to speak. "I live about a mile away. It's walkable but probably not a fun walk."

Chase spoke next. "Well, I'm only a few blocks from the school, but we would have to backtrack all the way there."

"I'm probably the closest now that I think about it," said Ebony.

"We live around the corner from each other, and we are further than Chase," said Shar, looking in the direction of where they would need to head to go near their homes.

"Yes, that's my mom's house. Remember, I live with my dad too." Ebony was so settled into her schedule that people forgot that she spent half her time with her mom and half the time with her dad. They had been divorced almost five years now, so the routine appeared to be almost second nature to Ebony at this point. She even had two sets of books from school so she didn't have to risk leaving things at one house or the other. Akiya was particularly impressed with Ebony's bedrooms. To help her feel more settled, her parents had decorated her bedroom at both houses exactly the same. This way, no matter which house she was at, she always felt like she was home.

"Well, what are we waiting for?" Akiya chimed in. She had already grabbed Ebony by the arm. The group started off toward Ebony's home with her dad.

Chapter Eight

"So, which way do we go?" asked Chase, grabbing his bag. While Shar and Akiya had spent plenty of time at Ebony's dad's house, none of the boys had ever been there. Chase didn't want to admit it, but he felt slightly excited about going to Ebony's house.

They initially started down the street in silence. Shar, never one to hold her tongue, said what everyone else was thinking. "Who would call the police on a bunch of kids?"

"I wish we could find out who did it." Marcus was relieved to get a chance to talk about what had happened.

"Well, it had to be someone who could see us," answered Shar. "Hey, Ebony, don't you have a telescope? Maybe we could set it up in your mom's office window, Chase. We could see if there are any windows with people lurking and being suspicious."

"We would be the people being suspicious." Terrence was finally feeling well enough to join the conversation. "Wouldn't trying to look into someone's window with a telescope be breaking some sort of laws?"

"I wouldn't mind the telescope idea at all." Marcus spoke confidently, always ready for an adventure. "But Auntie's office isn't toward the street, it's on the other side of the building."

Ebony wasn't too keen on using her telescope to commit a possible crime. She tried to think of a way to find out who made the call without using her telescope. And she wasn't about to remind them that she had two, one in each bedroom. They might get ideas for even more significant surveillance. "Maybe we can figure out how to get a copy of the 911 call. You always hear calls on the news. If they can get a recording, why can't we?"

"Maybe because we're kids?" asked Akiya, trying to be the voice of reason.

"What if they didn't know that we were kids?" asked Marcus.

"And how would they not know we were kids?"

"There are quite a few ways." Chase was ready to dive in. "We could use voice altering software. We could send the request via email and not mention that we were kids. If you use a proxy account from a foreign site and—"

"Are you insane?" Ebony was now sure the next time police cars showed up it might not be a terrible mistake with this kind of talk. "Do you know how many people go to jail for things like that?"

"How many?" asked Chase with a smile.

"A lot! I'm pretty sure I saw a video about it recently," Akiya chimed in.

"Source code or it didn't happen," answered Chase.

"What is that supposed to mean?"

Marcus put his hand on Chase's back. "You haven't heard him say this twenty times a day?" In his best Chase impression, Marcus began, "Video can be spliced and photos can be shopped. I need the source code before I believe the proof you got."

"Hey, it's true. Besides, using a proxy address isn't illegal unless you're trying to access illegal information. And police calls are public record. My dad even has a police scanner that tells you if they are going to big calls."

"Okay, and then what?" asked Akiya. "What happens if we do find out who made the call? Do we go up to their house and knock on the door? Do we send them a nasty letter?"

"Look, they did a dangerous thing. We could have gotten really hurt in that situation, especially if we would have run and something like that." Chase didn't look at anyone as he spoke. He wasn't blaming them for being scared and not knowing exactly what to do at the time.

"We have a right to know why someone decided to send the police after us when we weren't even doing anything wrong. This is my neighborhood. Chase and I come around here to fly my drone since there's that big grassy area next to my aunt's building. I don't want someone calling the cops every time I step outside. I mean really, we were doing our homework! That isn't a crime and someone tried to act like it was." Marcus didn't even realize he was yelling until Ebony's eyes got wide and she stepped back a bit.

"Sorry." His cheeks flushed, which was common when he realized people could tell just how upset he was. He was usually really good at taking it all in stride. But the unfairness of the situation was building started to pour out of his mouth at once. Chase knew exactly the feeling, this was another area where he and Marcus were so much alike.

They made their way up the driveway to the two-story home. The house was painted a soft yellow color with brown shutters and a brown front door with a small round window. The two windows on either side of the door had the blinds opened. There were several cars parked in the driveway and in front of the house.

"Hey, what's my mom doing here?" asked Shar.

"That's our car too," added Terrence.

"My mom said she was going to call everyone's parents, maybe they all decided to show up." Chase stopped by a big oak tree in front of the house and put his backpack down. Just then, the front door opened. A tall woman wearing pink leggings and an oversized shirt walked through the door.

"Mom!" Terrence looked like he was going to faint. "What are you wearing?"

"I was on my way to hot yoga when I got the call. You know tonight is hot yoga night. Anyway, I wanted to be here when you arrived. Are you okay?"

While Terrence's mother came toward him as if she was a mother eagle about to swoop up a baby eagle to try to keep it from tumbling out of the nest down a rocky cliff to its death, the others worked hard to suppress a giggle. Mainly because they knew their parents were all inside and were liable to be wearing something just as odd and ready to pounce on them with hugs and kisses as if they'd just returned from climbing Mt. Everest.

"What the heck is hot yoga?" Chase whispered to Marcus.

"I don't know—maybe something like fried ice cream. You know when things that are supposed to be opposites are put together. Wait, she didn't say yogurt, did she? I thought like instead of frozen yogurt she was going to eat hot yogurt, but that seems like a really bad idea. So I'm going to stick with I don't know."

Akiya chimed in, "Hot yoga is an exercise class. They do yoga but have the temperature of the room up really high to encourage sweating. People think it helps them lose more weight."

"I would think it would just make the room really stinky! I mean, my mom always gets mad when I come into the house all sweaty. Why would a bunch of people decide it would be a good idea to sweat even more?"

Terrence was wriggling like a snake to get out of the grasp of his mother and her loud workout attire. “Mom, we aren’t finished with the scavenger hunt. I’m fine, I just have to finish my homework.”

“Okay, I know you think you’re too old to get hugs from your mother! But I had to make sure you were okay. How is your stomach? Are you still sick?” His mom was looking at Terrence with concern.

“Mom, I’m fine. Homework, remember? I’m slowing the group down.” He was backing away to join the group.

“Alright. Now that I’ve seen you, I know you’re fine. I’ll wait for you inside.” With that, she bounded back toward the front door. She did a little jog on the steps before she went inside.

“Please don’t let her start exercising right here in the open,” moaned Terrence as he closed his eyes.

“Don’t worry, she went inside,” said Ebony. “And no need to be embarrassed, we all have parents. Besides, at least you aren’t going to have the awkward moment I will when we all go inside.”

"What do you mean?" asked Shar.

"My mom is here too!" said Ebony. She didn't talk often about her parents' divorce. They seemed to be cordial and no one had ever seen them be anything but kind to each other. But Ebony still looked a little tense, like she would rather close her eyes and pretend the world away right along with Terrence.

"Well, the adults will have to solve their own relationship problems and exercise issues. We have a clue to solve!" Marcus was unfolding the yellow paper again. "Head for the flowers and strike a pose. What in the world could that mean?"

"My dad has a couple of flower beds. There are those two beneath the windows in the front and a big one by the patio in the back," said Ebony.

"I wonder which one we start at," said Shar looking around.

Chase headed toward the bed of blue, yellow, and red tulips beneath the window on the right. He gently stepped between the flowers, kneeling down to see if there was something between the rows. Next, he glanced upward and started looking around the sides of the roof. He shrugged his shoulders, said, "Oh well," and then immediately started doing a bunch of crazy moves that looked like he was having fits. First, he put his arms above his head, bent his elbows, and swished his wrists from side to side. He then started putting his hands around his face like he was framing them in a picture.

"What in the world are you doing?" yelled Marcus through tears of laughter. "You didn't eat any of those flowers when you went over there, did you? I think you might be having some sort of reaction!"

"No, you dolt!" Chase shouted back. "I'm doing exactly what the clue said to do. I'm striking a pose in the flowers."

Shar pulled out her phone and started taking pictures. "I have no idea if he's doing it right, but this is worth it anyway." She was recording video and texting the other two girls at the same time.

Terrence was looking from one flower bed to the other. "Anything happening yet?" asked Chase as he kept doing the most ridiculous poses he could think of.

"Nope," answered Terrence, doing his best to hold back a laugh.

"Ebony, what are those?" Akiya was pointing to cameras on either side of the porch.

"Oh, they're my dad's security cameras. They go around the entire house. There's a big computer screen on the wall in his office and he can see everything happening on the cameras," answered Ebony.

Chase immediately stopped posing. "Wait a minute? You mean everyone in that house could be staring at a screen watching me right now?"

"You mean I didn't have to take pictures? I could have just gone inside and recorded from a big screen?" asked Shar.

Marcus spotted the yellow envelope just behind the flowerpot on the front porch. Ebony walked over and picked it up. "Wow!" Her eyes were wide, and a broad smile went across her face.

"What is it? What does it say?" asked Shar, who wasn't sure if Ebony was going to laugh or cry from her expression.

Ebony began to read so quickly they almost couldn't understand the words as they were tumbling out of her mouth. "The video-based home security system was invented by Marie Van Britton Brown and her husband Albert Brown. They received patent number 3,482,037 in 1966. Mrs. Brown said the inspiration for her invention was how long it would take police to arrive at a house after being called to a residence. She also did not like to open the door without knowing who it was on the other side. The security system she invented allowed the monitor to be in a different room and was controlled via a wireless system."

Akiya was almost jumping up and down with excitement. "Yes! We made that!"

Chase was smiling just as broadly as Ebony. "I had no idea. Go ahead, Mrs. Van Britton Brown!"

Marcus chimed in, “Slightly ironic that she invented this security system because the police arrived too slow, they seemed to find us pretty quickly.”

“Let’s not interrupt the celebration. What’s our next clue?” Terrence wanted to change the subject, even though he was having the same thoughts as Marcus. Chase had resumed his striking a pose dance back in front of the camera system. Akiya took out the piece of paper to read the next clue.

Look how far you have come, but you are not done yet
Thankfully, I am around so that you won’t forget
I help the flowers to bloom rightly and the grass to stay lush
But I keep the flow in check, we don’t want the ground to be mush
I am a few minutes here and there, no more than twice a day
I don’t interrupt work, but sometimes I do help with play

#

"I have no idea what this is talking about." Terrence kept reading and re-reading the clue as if more would appear if he concentrated hard enough.

Everyone looked at Akiya, she was the puzzle queen. Shar nodded her head up and down, hoping that would help to propel some thoughts into Akiya's mind. "I'm thinking, I'm thinking. It must be some sort of gardening tool, right? Ebony, does your dad have some sort of a shed?"

"Yes, but I don't know what in the shed would help with play. That was a part of the clue as well. What helps plants and trees but also helps with play?"

"Mud." Chase had decided to stop striking poses and join the conversation. "Well, dirt anyway. Plants need dirt. Little kids play in dirt. Some kids eat dirt. Did I ever tell you about the time Marcus tried to eat dirt when we were little?"

"I didn't try to eat dirt! I have much more refined taste than that! It was mud. A mud pie that I had taken the time to prepare with only the finest of poaceae and gramineae, as well as some common Bermuda grass for good measure!"

"Of course, why didn't I think of that?" Ebony was now headed back toward the house.

"I know she is a woman of few words, but does it seem like I might have oversold the mud pie thing and now she wants to make one for herself?" Marcus followed behind Ebony with a look of both curiosity and anticipation that someone might be as daring as he or Chase usually were when it came to performing the unexpected.

"No, silly!" Ebony had stopped in front of a small metal pipe that was sticking out of the ground. "The sprinkler system!"

"Oh, yeah. You know, that makes much more sense than you deciding to wait until now to start eating dirt."

By this time, the rest of the group had joined them, and Terrence spotted the yellow envelope near another sprinkler head that was closer to the garage door. He opened the letter and began to read loudly, "Joseph Smith received patent #601,065 in 1898 for an improved sprinkler head. It is a design still in use today."

"Wow, I can't believe we're still using something that was patented over 100 years ago! That's amazing." Terrence was now down on the ground, face so close to the sprinkler it was almost like he could taste it. He loved contraptions and designs that would move and interact with the environment. It was one of the reasons he could spend hours in his room putting together intricate models of cars and planes. He gently removed the casing and looked at the various gears and wondered just how Joseph Smith decided which elements needed improvement to be so good we still wanted to use them in this century. He thought about how many things were made possible due to automatic sprinklers. All the food grown in gardens and farms around the world. All the lush grass that could be seen in suburban neighborhoods. All the fields at community parks. Not to mention all the hours of fun that could be had while playing in sprinklers on hot summer days.

Automatic sprinklers also do a lot for the environment. You can control when they turn on, making sure they are used at the most efficient times of the day and ensuring water isn't lost to evaporation. You can control the intervals in which they are on, ensuring water is not being used for too long and not being wasted due to overuse. The automatic sprinkler really was an amazing invention.

Chapter Nine

"No resting just yet, we still have another clue!" Chase had reached out a hand and was pulling Terrence to his feet.

#

You're almost there, you're almost done
I hope you learned a lot and had some fun
This last thing you will find today
Is how you work before you play
You saw how we use water so that we can grow
This is the next step that happens after you sow

#

Everyone looked at each other, hoping someone had a clue of where to start. "Okay, we made it this far—let's see if we can figure out this last clue." Chase was reading over the clue one more time.

Akiya looked back through her notes she had been taking. With everything that had happened with the police, she realized she hadn't taken enough notes and didn't want to forget anything important before it was time to start writing their report. "This has been so much fun, I'm almost sad it's our last clue."

Marcus snorted. "Akiya, it's school work, of course you aren't ready for it to end!"

"Well, I'm not usually one for a lot of extra work, but I wouldn't mind this lasting a bit longer either. I really learned a lot." Terrence had found himself back at the sprinkler head and looked as if he was wishing he could take an even closer look inside at some of the working pieces.

"Well, I'm hungry and a little tired, so we're going to have to wrap this up." Shar was headed over to Chase.

"You really think a house full of our parents doesn't have snacks? There will be snacks. But let's figure this out. This is the work before play, what's out here that is about work?" Chase was now turning around in a circle trying to see if anything in particular jumped out at him.

"Well, we just found a sprinkler and that was about watering grass. What else do you need for grass to grow?" Marcus decided to answer his own question. "I mean to grow grass you just need water and sunlight. Certainly, we're not going to say a Black American invented the sun. I would think that belonged to someone like Zeus." He was now laughing hard at his own joke. Ebony, however, did not think this was funny at all.

"Zeus! Are you kidding? Ra, the Egyptian god, is the one who would be considered the inventor of the sun. I mean, the Greek god Apollo rides the chariot that drives the sun. But we're talking about inventors here. So, I would go with Ra. I guess the Yoruba god Olorun might be a candidate as well. No. That doesn't sound right. It would have to be Mawu. Of course, why didn't I think of Mawu first?"

When Ebony looked up, everyone was staring at her with their mouths open. There were only two topics that could get Ebony talking—astronomy and mythology. When she realized everyone was looking at her, she blushed and smiled hard. "Sorry!"

"Hey, don't be sorry at all. I could hear you talk about sun gods all day. But I sort of think Marcus was just being funny," laughed Shar.

"Totally being funny. I know Zeus didn't invent the sun. I just don't know how we're going to find a human that has anything to do with photosynthesis taking place."

"I don't think it's about growing the grass. That seems to be already established in the clue. What would come next that would be work?" Akiya placed her hand on her chin.

"Oh, I know what it is!" exclaimed Ebony as she headed toward the shed. She gently opened the door and pushed through the various tools and equipment, disappearing into the dimly lit shed. She was back out the door with a contraption that looked to the others like some sort of torture device. It had a long wooden and metal handle. At the end of the handle was a long, bronze looking cylinder barrel with sharp blades that looked to intertwine with one another.

"What is that?" asked Terrence, coming in closer for a look.

"It's a lawn mower," stated Ebony, matter of factly.

"I know it's a lawn mower. Why would you be using one without a motor, and a comfortable seat, and a cup holder?" Marcus was now pretending to sit on an invisible lawn mower.

"If you need all those gadgets that's fine, but this one works just as well," answered Ebony.

"You use this?" Chase lifted his eyebrows in amazement.

"Why wouldn't she use this? Do you think girls don't also mow the lawn?" Shar was now staring at Chase and shaking her head in displeasure.

"Of course, I know girls mow the lawn, but that thing looks ancient."

"Well, yes, it is old. It belonged to my grandmother. But it still works. Let me show you." Shar handed Akiya the yellow envelope that had been attached to the lawnmower when she grabbed it. She then put her hands into the handles that were at the top of the lawnmower and gave it a strong shove with her arms. As she moved forward, the blades began to rotate. Everyone could see a patch of cut grass behind her as she moved along.

"Let me try!" Marcus, not usually one for volunteering for chores, found himself once again wanting to help. "Wow, this is hard work. How long does it take you to do the entire yard?"

"It takes a while, but I usually do it in sections. If we need to get it done quickly, there is an electric mower in the shed as well. However, I always use this for the edges next to the flower beds. It is perfect for getting close to your cut line without crossing it."

"Impressive." Chase was watching while Terrence was happily taking his turn cutting the grass now. "But I'll take a riding mower anyway!"

"Yeah, but think about how much pollution this keeps away. Plus, you wouldn't be using any fossil fuels. It is hard work, but this it totally green energy as well." Terrence stopped pushing for a minute and asked, "Akiya, who does it say invented this?"

Akiya started reading. "Congratulations! You found your last clue of the scavenger hunt. John Albert Burr invented the push rotary blade lawnmower, receiving patent number 624,749 in the year 1899. Mr. Burr was a former slave and his knack for engineering was well noticed. He attended engineering classes at a private university. His classes were paid for by wealthy Black activists. Combining his natural talents and education, Mr. Burr went on to obtain several patents for home gardening and other devices."

"Wow, we made this?" Marcus was piping up again, ready for his turn back on the lawnmower. "I honestly had no idea so many things we use and encounter every day were created or improved to our modern form by Black Americans."

#

They all headed toward Ebony's front door and were surprised by all of the faces staring back at them as they walked into the living room. There seemed to be too few places to sit for all of the adults who were gathered there and it was surprising to see some even sitting on the floor. There was an awkward silence in the air, which made everyone twitch a bit. Mr. Sparks stood up and went to the center of the living room. He placed his glass of water on the table and began to speak. "Well, since you six have come into the house, I take it that you found all of the clues. I want to start by saying congratulations and job well done! The second thing I want to do is apologize."

"Apologize for what?" Marcus and Chase both spoke at the same time.

"Yeah, this was great! We had a blast." Shar was now standing next to the cousins. After she spoke, she started to look around as if her mind began to swirl. The others knew Shar had to begin asking herself a million questions. Had they actually done something wrong? What could the apology possibly be for? Mr. Sparks started by saying congratulations, was this one of those times when people thank you for participating but you didn't actually win? Now she was regretting saying they had a good time. Did they have a good time doing the scavenger hunt wrong? Shar hated disappointing adults.

"Did we do something wrong?" Terrence must have been thinking the same thing as Shar. He spoke the words quietly and let them hang in the air.

"You all did absolutely nothing wrong. However, I feel like I should have anticipated that someone might not understand what you all were doing and call the police. I should have prepared you for that." Mr. Sparks was looking at each of them, an air of sadness in his eyes.

"Wait, why should I have to be warned about going around my own neighborhood?" Marcus spoke with a bit more force than he anticipated.

"Exactly!" Chase was now on his feet. "We were at Mom's building. Marcus and I go there all the time. Ebony lives within walking distance of that street. We all have walked or ridden our bikes to the ice cream shop down the street from there. What exactly could you have said, Uncle?"

"Chase." The name echoed as two very similar voices said his name at the same time. Not only did Mrs. Thornton and Mrs. Sparks look exactly alike, they sounded exactly alike. It was clear that Chase and Marcus got their similar looks from their mothers being identical twins. This also explained their closeness as they were raised so close together. Often times, Marcus and Chase operated more like brothers than cousins. Both boys saw their aunts as almost a second mother. It wasn't surprising that both Mrs. Thornton and Mrs. Sparks were moving toward Chase at the same time.

Mrs. Thornton was the first to speak. "Chase, you and Marcus can still come to our building at any time. You will always be welcomed there and we will make sure that you are safe. We are already putting things in place to try to keep this from happening again."

"Like finding out who did it and letting them know they aren't allowed to call the police on kids just doing their homework?" Marcus had a serious look on his face. His usual cheery and mischievous smile was gone, and for the first time, everyone could see just how hurt he was.

"It was against the law." Akiya was looking out the window as she spoke. She never wanted to be one to argue with adults. "You can't make a false report to police officers. That person broke the law and they should be arrested."

"They won't be arrested. That person isn't going to get in trouble at all. Even with the video." Shar was looking more defiantly at all of the adults.

"That is why we are all here talking to you now, Shar." Mr. Sparks spoke in a gentle voice. "The young lady who recorded the video uploaded it to a few social media sites. So far, it has received 10,000 views. Word of what happened is going to get around and we want to make sure you all are prepared."

A pit dropped in each of their stomachs. What in the world were they going to have to face? "But we didn't do anything wrong." Ebony looked up with tears in her eyes and ran to her father. He placed his arms around her. Her mother, who had been sitting in a chair in the corner, walked over and hugged her as well. Ebony felt herself relax.

"You all have support. No one is saying you did anything wrong. So far, all the comments are supportive. They said you did everything right, and you did. We are very proud of all of you. We just want you to know that it isn't a private matter. There are people in the community, at school, and other places who might know what's going on. We just want you to know that you don't have to answer any questions from anyone that you don't want to." Mr. Sparks was now patting Terrence on the back. It appeared the color was draining from the boy's face. It appeared as if everything started to flood back to him. It was clear he was wondering if now everyone was going to know that he wasn't brave and calm like Marcus and Chase. In fact, he'd gotten so overwhelmed he'd actually thrown up. Was everyone going to be laughing at him now? He felt everyone's eyes look toward him and the room began to spin in his head. If he didn't do something soon, he might end up throwing up again.

"The scavenger hunt was fun!" Terrence saw everyone's face light up. Maybe the focus wouldn't be on him for long.

"I didn't want it to end." Akiya was now away from the window and walking to the center of the room. "I even checked out the book, *Clotel*. I can't wait to read it."

"All the things we learned about today and you're most excited about a book?" Chase was laughing and shaking his head.

"Well, what was your favorite part?" asked Akiya.

Chase immediately resumed the dance poses he had been doing in the garden. "Finding out that a Black American was the one who invented a system that allowed me to show my best moves to a crowd of adoring fans looking at a television screen."

"Dude, it's a security system, not a television studio." Marcus was laughing hard now, his signature smile back on full display.

"It has dual purposes!" retorted Chase.

"Should we call up Marie Van Britton Brown and ask her?" Mr. Sparks laughed.

"My favorite was the pencil sharpener that was invented by John Lee Love," added Shar.

"For the name, right? You love it because it was a guy named Love that invented it?" Chase was now pretending to wink and blush at the same time.

"Absolutely not!" Shar was indignant but came down quickly. "I liked it because of the simplicity, but think about how important it is. We use so many small things every day and we rarely even think about where they came from. Who had the idea? How did that person decide to make it better? I wonder what it's like to think like an inventor."

"Great points, Shar." Mr. Sparks was walking back to the middle of the room. "Actually, that was what I hoped you all would get out of this experience. That anyone can think like an inventor, and we need you to think like inventors.

"My favorite was the sprinkler head." Terrence piped up quickly. At first, he had started this conversation just to change the subject. However, he really did want to talk about it now. "It's so important when you think about it. When we use sprinklers properly, we're actually protecting the environment. We aren't wasting water unnecessarily and they are particularly helpful when we are trying to grow plants and vegetables. I was looking at the design of the sprinkler and there were so many intricate pieces. It was fun to close my eyes and think about how it all worked together."

"What do you mean close your eyes to see how it worked together?" interrupted Shar. She wasn't trying to be rude, she was just really interested in what Terrence was saying.

"It's actually a part of being dyslexic. While there are a lot of things I don't like about dyslexia, like my trouble with spelling, there are some good things as well. Come to find out, one of the reasons I tend to reverse numbers and letters when I write is because my mind can flip things around as I see them, even on flat surfaces. I used to hate it, but it actually really helps when I'm building models and figuring out how machines work." Terrence was smiling now. It wasn't often he got a chance to speak openly about being dyslexic. It was actually something he used to try to hide. However, Global Academy prided itself on learning by working with others and his dyslexia was hard to hide during group projects. Thankfully, no one made fun of him, he was even surprised to learn he wasn't the only one in class with dyslexia.

Ebony's dad walked over and gave Terrence a pat on the back. "Did you know that a lot of famous people are dyslexic? Lots of inventors have dyslexia, for many of the reasons you mentioned. Maybe a group of kids will be going on a scavenger hunt looking for something that you invented in the not-so-distant future. Terrence smiled. It felt good to hear someone talk about the things he could do and not the things that he couldn't.

"My turn!" said Ebony. She actually raised her hand but quickly put it back down and laughed to herself a bit. She so often wanted to follow the rules that she sometimes put rules in place that weren't quite there. "My favorite was learning about Garrett Morgan and his invention of the yellow signal for the traffic light. Even though he improved someone else's idea instead of inventing something completely new, it was very creative. I can hardly imagine how many lives he saved with his invention. In fact, it's kind of weird that they didn't start with the yellow light being a part of the traffic light in the first place."

"You would be surprised at how many new things come to market that aren't quite safe when they're first sold." Terrence's mom was speaking. "My entire job is about finding risks and determining what the chances are that something not so good could come out of an invention."

"So, what kind of risk would you put on Lightning and Thunder over here?" Mrs. Thornton laughed.

"You know you like our pranks," said Chase. "Mrs. Kingston, how do you decide that? Do you just use a computer to come up with it? Are you a computer programmer?"

"I do use a computer, but it involves more than that. My official job title is an actuary. We help companies figure out what the chances are that something will work out well or something will go terribly wrong. We help them figure out if an idea, a product, or even a service is worth the risk. Some risk is good, but there is a point where the chances of something going wrong are too high to be worth it. I help to figure out where that point is."

"Like, for instance, if you were trying to make a basketball shot into a trashcan with a half full carton of milk?" Shar pretended to be asking the question in all seriousness, even though she was looking at Chase through the corner of her eye.

"It was not a half full carton of milk, it was half empty." Chase was nodding his head at his cleverness. Until he looked at his mom who seemed to be determining that something happened with milk that Chase hadn't disclosed. He quickly ducked behind Marcus.

Chapter Ten

"Well, there were so many cool things that I found out today I can't decide which was my favorite."

"Don't worry, honey. I have some special things to show you that might help you decide." Mrs. Sparks had a mischievous smirk on her face.

"Oh, he's going to love the next part of his adventure," said Mrs. Thornton.

"Wait, what are you two talking about?" asked Marcus, who started to have a worried look on his face.

"No need to fret, young man, let's head home," replied Mrs. Sparks.

Everyone began to gather their things to leave. The STEAM Chasers decided to meet early before class the next day so they could figure out what they were going to do to put together their final project. They had gathered a lot of great information, but they still needed to write the paper and think of a creative way to present their findings to their classmates. They decided that each person would come up with a presentation idea and they would vote on whose sounded the most fun and interesting.

"Do you think anyone at school will have seen the video?" Terrence clearly tried to force the worry out of his mind. It was clear he just couldn't shake the idea of everyone seeing just how worried he had been. He didn't know if people would make fun of him for being so scared that he made himself sick. It didn't seem fair that such a fun day had such a dark shadow in the midst of it. He wanted to concentrate on the fun he had today, but the fear was also in his mind.

"Terrence, don't worry about it. We'll figure out who made that call. I've been thinking of a plan." This information didn't make Terrence feel better. As uncomfortable as he was about Chase trying to hack into the police system, Marcus deciding that he had come up with a plan made him feel even more nervous.

"And what, by chance, is your plan?" Clearly Shar was just as concerned as Terrence.

"Drone power!" Marcus was nodding his head and smiling. He had gotten quite good with flying drones. He'd gotten his first drone for his birthday when he was nine. He had been hooked ever since. He had even managed to build his own drone out of Legos and motors. But his specialty had become reconnaissance drones. That was a fancy word for spy drones. Marcus was the youngest kid in the area with a drone license. His city had passed an ordinance that anyone who flew drones at a certain altitude must have a license, and Marcus had gone all the way to the city council to have them clarify the language that there was no minimum age for a license as long as you could pass the test. He was so excited about passing that test, he even studied for and passed the test to become a Ham radio operator. This was helpful for the few times he had lost his drone on flights and could send a message out to others via radio to be on the lookout.

Everyone said it went along with his nickname of being the Lightning. Quick and leaving only a slight flash as it passed overhead. He was such a good drone pilot, he could even race them against other drone pilots through obstacle courses. However, Marcus had always stayed on the up-and-up with his drone usage. He was never one to cross the line because he knew he was being an example for other young people who might also want to get their drone license.

"Marcus, don't." Akiya was reaching out for his shoulder. "Do you want to end up in jail? Like for real this time. You're supposed to leave your spying to squirrels and birds, not people."

"So Ebony can't use her telescope, Chase can't hack into the system, and now I can't fly my drone. How in the world are we supposed to find out any information?" Marcus was yelling as quietly as possible in order not to let any of their parents overhear the conversation.

"Let's just give it twenty-four hours. We'll come up with a plan that won't lead to any of us getting arrested for real this time," said Ebony.

While the others walked on ahead of them, Chase and Marcus gave each other the look. This was the look when they were both on the same page and knew they might have to think outside the lines a little bit. Besides, they weren't doing anything wrong. They were the victims. This wasn't them being bad, this was justice. They didn't need to say a word, just a head nod would do. They had been talking about seeing if they could program a drone to carry out specific tasks, maybe it was time they started to go forward with that plan after all.

Marcus didn't say much on the drive home. He was too busy thinking about how he would go forward with the plan. It wasn't until they pulled into the driveway that he realized he had forgotten to do his chores that day. No worries—he had been doing homework all day. His parents couldn't possibly be upset. School work was always a priority and he could always do his chores in the morning before school. Except he had already planned on meeting the other STEAM Chasers before school. Well, he would do his chores after school the next day. Either way, they would definitely be done some time before the weekend. After he unbuckled his seatbelt and started opening the car door, his mother reached back and handed him an envelope. "Oh, your adventure isn't over, young man. I have some additional clues for you inside the house."

"Okay. I thought my homework was already done, but I guess learning a few more things wouldn't hurt." He laughed as he took the envelope out of his mother's hands. He could have sworn his mom and dad gave each other a quick wink.

It seems that others long ago had already seen your fate

They created some things you will need before it is too late

Make sure you work hard at finding what you need to become a winner
You will need to seek them and use them before you can have dinner

#

Marcus looked at his parents. “What is this?”

“Oh, there are a few more things you need to find. Surely you didn’t think you all had found everything invented by Black Americans that we use in our everyday lives? Nope, you all barely scratched the surface.” His father was now openly laughing.

Marcus had no idea what was going on, but he’d had so much fun finding the other clues, that he was ready to extend the adventure. He walked up the porch and opened the front door. What could be something that he needed? Well, he was kind of hungry, so maybe what he needed was a snack! He went directly to the kitchen to see if maybe there was a plate of lasagna waiting for him. He looked on the counter and saw that nothing was there. He also noticed pieces of cereal on the floor that he had dropped that morning and not bothered to pick up. He'd been a little heavy handed and quite a bit had ended up on the floor and not in his bowl. Oh well, he would make sure he took care of it, but just not yet. He looked around the room again, wondering if his clue was hiding in there somewhere. Nothing seemed obvious. He was now realizing the other part of his clue, he couldn't eat dinner until he solved the riddle. Okay, maybe it was in his bedroom. He walked down the hall and into his room. Unfortunately, he had to step over a few dirty socks. That was another thing he would take care of later. "Mom, I'm not seeing any clues. Are they in my room?"

His mother and father came around the corner and looked into his room. "Certainly, you looked harder than this when you all were out exploring today," said his mother. Marcus left the room and headed back toward the kitchen. As he passed the laundry room, he noticed something yellow out of the corner of his eye.

He opened the door and saw the envelope. It was attached to a mop. He opened it slowly, scared of what he would find.

Congratulations! You missed a few chores before you left the house today. Never fear, there are several inventions by Black Americans that are here to help you on your journey. What journey? The journey of a week of extra chores! Here we have the mop. This design was invented by Thomas W. Stewart. He received patent number 499,402 in 1893. Next to it you see the dust pan, invented by Lloyd P. Ray who received patent number 587,607 in 1897. For your added pleasure, your new chores this week will include doing all the laundry. Wonderfully enough, George T. Sampson was looking out for you when he invented a version of the clothes dryer with patent number 476,416 in 1892. To round things off you will be using an invention by Sarah Boone—an improvement for the ironing board for which she received patent number 473,653 in 1892.

Chapter Eleven

Chase was feeling both nervous and excited as he headed toward his bedroom. His parents kept trying to ask him about his day all through dinner. Usually, he was happy to talk to them about the various happenings of one adventure or another. Of course, there were occasional times when he left out some details, but for the most part, his parents were laid back and they were always supportive. Of course, it was hard not to show that something was in the process of being planned. Marcus kept texting him the entire time. First, he texted to ask who cooked dinner. It was his mom, Chase's dad normally cooked on the weekends when Mrs. Thornton was most likely to be showing homes or looking for properties that she wanted to rehab and flip. She had a great eye for knowing that a little TLC would make a house more appealing. She said she loved the art and architecture of it all, plus she loved running the numbers to see if a project would make sense to invest in. Chase still didn't quite understand when his mom talked about art and math as if they were almost one and the same. "Patterns, Chase. Beautiful patterns when done right come out perfectly balanced. Especially algebra." Then she would start talking about how Chase would just love algebra and he really thought she had lost her marbles. Ebony was the only kid he knew who loved numbers, but even she didn't wax poetic about algebra. Chase had finally determined if his mom talked anymore about things being perfectly balanced, it would be proof she was the villain Thanos and he would be looking for a new place, or maybe even a new planet, to live.

Chase texted back that they were eating lasagna. Yup, same for Marcus. They were keeping a running tally of how many times their identical twin mothers cooked the exact same meal on the exact same day, even when they didn't plan it. His mom was a good cook, but Chase still preferred when his dad made dinner. Chase's dad was a computer programmer who always tried to work while he was cooking dinner. This meant that, at least once a week, he would burn it and end up having to order pizza. Chase guessed that was why his parents were so unfazed by his own programming obsessions. He was, in fact, just like his dad.

Marcus's texts eventually moved on to whether or not he was going to start writing code for the drone. He texted back that he would have started already if Marcus hadn't kept bothering him. Finally, he was finished with dinner, and his parents were sufficiently satisfied with the conversation, that he was dismissed from the table to go to his room. They didn't know what he planned on working on. Before long, he had both his desktop and his laptop going full speed. His mom often teased him, saying that English wasn't his first language, it was the programming language of Python. After about an hour, there was a knock on his bedroom door. Surely Marcus hadn't decided to bug him in person. He got up and opened the door. "Hey, son, mind if I come in?"

"Sure, Dad." Chase knew this was about to be a serious conversation. When his dad knocked and asked for permission to come in, that was always a sign that something important needed to be discussed. "You look like you have some serious programming going on. Anything you care to share with me?" His dad looked at him with those piercing eyes. The ones that were gentle and pleading with Chase to talk to him honestly. "No, nothing that I would like to share." Chase emphasized the word "like", which meant he wasn't actually lying at the moment.

"Chase, I know when you and Marcus start communicating like this, you have something big up your sleeve. I also know you, better than you think I do. I know you might not understand, Chase, but I am going to ask you not to do this." His dad looked at him more sternly now.

"Do what?" Chase tried to sound innocent.

"Try to find out who made that phone call to the police. I don't know what you have planned—whether hacking into the police station or some other crazy ideas. But I'm going to need you not to do whatever scheme the two of you have come up with."

Wow, his dad did know him really well. Chase went to speak in protest, but his dad kept talking. "I came to you to ask you not to do it because I don't think you will fail—in fact, I know you won't fail. I know whatever you plan, it is going to work. But this isn't your job. It's my job, it's your mom's job, it's your aunt and uncle's job. I know this happened to you all and it wasn't fair. I am not going to sit here and pretend like you shouldn't be angry, I get that. Chase, you have got to trust me on this one."

It seemed like his dad was about to say something else, but right then, the smoke detector went off with a loud, hissing, shrieking noise that made Chase cover his ears. "I know, my brownies. Look, son—no playing the Avengers of Cyberspace right now. Let me go before I burn the house down." His dad ran out the door, and Chase could hear his mother yelling, "What in the world are you doing? I swear, Jabari, I am going to start banning you from the kitchen!"

Chase was convinced he was given his father's first name as his middle name so that when his mom yelled, "Jabari," it would cover both of them since usually yelling out their name would accurately identify each as doing something that put the house in some sort of danger. Like the time Chase tried to program an automatic locking system on the front door and they couldn't open it for a week because he forgot the password that he used to set it. He probably would have gotten into a lot more trouble if his mom wasn't preoccupied with his dad also setting the BBQ grill on fire because he forgot about the salmon and pineapple he had put on for dinner that day. Even the fire department was impressed at his dad's ability to melt down to ash a piece of equipment that was designed to actually hold fire in the first place.

Chase was thinking about this as he flopped down on his bed. He looked over at the code running on his laptop. There was so much to think about. He knew his dad was right, but Marcus had good points as well. He started to think about the other STEAM Chasers. Terrence, Shar, Ebony, and Akiya, none of them were okay with the plan. For something this big and this important, everyone needed to be on the same page. He and Marcus were always a team, but could they be team players with others as well? Who knew just doing your homework would turn into something so crazy?

This all felt like an unfair situation to be in and Chase was frustrated that he had to spend any time trying to figure out what to do. As he closed his eyes to go to sleep, he wondered if any of the inventors he had learned about that day faced things such as this. Some of them were getting patents in the late 1800s, certainly they faced bigger issues than a fake call to the police. He fell asleep hoping he could muster the same type of courage he was sure they had to show as well. He knew whatever decision he made, someone from the STEAM Chasers would be disappointed. He was hoping that he made the right decision.

Chapter Twelve

"Really, Chase? You're admitting defeat without even trying?" Marcus was upset but trying to be nice. He really did understand the difficult position that Chase was in, and he knew he probably would have made the same decision.

"It isn't defeat to make a good decision." Akiya chimed in quickly.

"Marcus, my dad asked me to trust him, and my mom, plus your parents. I think we should give them a chance. If we aren't satisfied with what they come up with, then we enact our plan. Okay?" Chase really hoped this would win Marcus over, or at least buy them some time.

"Fine, I will concede to give the amateurs some time. But if they haven't done something significant by the time we finish this project, Plan B—which should have been Plan A—will go into full effect." He reached out for Chase's arm. "Blood pact?"

"Marcus, are you insane?" Shar was looking at Marcus as if he had two heads. "Why can't hacking into police headquarters or programming drones be plan E or F or Z?"

"Shar, I get it. You're scared. Fine. But I think people should be held accountable for ruining our day." Marcus was surprised that Shar wasn't more upset about what happened.

"We spent an entire day going around the city. We got introduced to ten amazing Black inventors. We had fun discovering new things. And instead of spending our time working on our projects, we've been talking about one buzzard-headed person who tried to ruin our day," answered Shar.

"Actually, I learned about fourteen amazing Black inventors," Marcus beamed at her. "Apparently, Black

Americans had a hand in inventing the mop, the dust pan, the clothes dryer, and the ironing board." He went on to tell them about his own private scavenger hunt.

"That is so amazing!" Ebony smiled.

"You think it's amazing that I have to wash, dry, and iron my dad's underwear for an entire week?" Marcus was looking at her with one eyebrow raised.

"Dude, your dad makes you iron his underwear?" asked Terrence with a look of both shock and horror.

"Okay, maybe not iron, but you get how traumatic the whole laundry thing is for me, right?"

Ebony jumped back into the conversation. "I'll admit that extra chores are no fun. But that is still really cool that we now know of even more inventions by Black Americans. I can't wait to share this with the class."

"Okay, who came with ideas for our presentation?"

Absolutely no one was surprised when Akiya was the first to raise her hand. She had the *Clotel* book sitting in front of her on her desk. "We should present something that we can patent!" She was so excited, the words tumbled out of her mouth instead of flowing smoothly.

"I'm sorry, I must have misheard you. Did you really just recommend that we go forward with the puppy army?" asked Marcus. He and Chase gave each other a high five.

"Akiya, it was bad enough being a part of a viral video showing me puke on the sidewalk. I would rather not have another encounter with the police because I tried to raise an army." Terrence's face was glowing hot with embarrassment just thinking about it.

"I wasn't recommending Marcus' puppy army." Akiya was determined not to let her enthusiasm fade. "We've just learned so much about patents, I thought we could try to put something together that would be worthy of a patent on our own."

"Create our own thing to impact everyday lives? That might be pretty neat!" Feeling better about not raising an army, Terrence was getting excited himself.

"But what would we invent?" asked Chase.

"I have an idea." Ebony was standing up at the end of the table. "What if we make something that could help other kids who might find themselves in the position we were in? Look, getting stopped by the police was pretty scary. If Marcus and Chase weren't there, I wouldn't have known what to do. What if we put our heads together and came up with something that would help kids in that situation?"

There was a long pause as everyone contemplated Ebony's idea. Shar looked at her and smiled. "Let's do it! Why go through a situation like that and not have something good come out of the other side?"

Mrs. Worthington entered the class and told everyone they could spend the entire morning working in their groups. This was perfect for the STEAM Chasers as they spent the time dividing up the work and continuing to bring out new ideas to make the presentation interesting. They hoped the rest of the class would get as excited about the things they learned as they were. They also couldn't wait to hear what other groups had found.

While everyone was working feverishly with their groups, they didn't even hear the classroom door swing open. Terrence was the first to look up as Principal Davis walked in with a smile. "Is this a good time, Mrs. Worthington?"

"Oh yes, come on in, Principal Davis. Class, your attention, please. I know you are working hard, but Principal Davis has an announcement to make."

It wasn't unusual for Principal Davis to show up in one class or another. It was unusual for him to make announcements. Everyone took their seats and looked at him in anticipation. "I have some exciting news for everyone. You all have been invited to not only present your latest group projects to each other but to the entire school and community. You will be presenting in three weeks at the Oxland Building. We are all looking forward to each of your presentations." With those words, Principal Davis turned and left.

Each group started talking feverishly with each other in excitement. Akiya looked at Chase. "Isn't the

Oxland Building where your mother's real estate office is? We all went there, right?"

Terrence jumped into the conversation. "Yeah, that's where we got the clue for Alexander Miles and his invention of the automatic elevator doors."

Chase and Marcus both looked at each other in confusion. "My mom never said anything about us presenting at her business. I have no idea where this all came from."

Ebony said quietly, "All the more reason why it would have been a bad idea to try to use telescopes or drones or hacking to find out who made that phone call. Can you imagine if we would have gotten caught snooping around the very area where the whole school was supposed to be?"

"I hate to say I told you so," said Shar.

"You didn't say I told you so!" snapped Chase.

"I'm pretty sure I did!" she retorted.

"Source code or it didn't happen!" He sat back in his chair and smiled.

"Just don't go hacking into anything around there, Chase. Please." Terrence was looking serious. He did not want to do anything that might have a chance of getting them negative exposure.

"Well, now we really have to make sure we have a great project." Shar was picking up the notes Akiya had written. "Let's start dividing up the tasks to see who will do what." Shar took charge and gave people their assignments. Terrence and Ebony got to work drawing sketches for the model. They decided to make a prototype that would be as close to the real thing as possible. Marcus and Akiya would work on ensuring their invention linked back to as many inventors as they learned about as possible. Chase and Shar would work together on the presentation to truly bring the invention to life for the audience. All the other groups looked to be just as busy.

Chapter Thirteen

“Mom, how can you not know the details about what’s going on? It’s happening at your building.” Chase couldn’t believe his mother had no clue. She just kept saying that all she heard was that his class was invited to present. However, he knew there had to be more to the story when his mother asked him before bed what he planned on wearing to the event. “Why do you care what I’m wearing? I mean, I can promise you that I won’t stink, but other than that, I have no idea.” Chase thought feigning the possibility of walking out of the house in his worst clothes might move his mother to give him some details. Just to see if he could push her even further, he added, “I might wear those jeans with the hole in the knee. They're only a little too small, but they are my favorite, and I want to make sure I'm comfortable in case I get nervous. I might wear my lucky shirt too. It's in the dirty clothes hamper? Did I promise I wouldn't stink? Maybe I can only promise that the bottom half of me won't stink."

He saw his mother twitch a little, but she composed herself quickly and answered, "Well, at least wear a nice tie so that a small part of you looks put together." With that quip, it was official, she wasn't budging.

Chase went back to his room to get dressed. Marcus had already texted him three times trying to see if he could get any answers from his mom. He finally texted back that maybe Marcus should ask his mother, since she might be caught off guard. They had read that twins could have a telepathic bond, maybe Mrs. Sparks knew the details by mind melding with Mrs. Thornton unconsciously. They both knew Akiya would tell them such telepathic connections were urban legend and not true, but they were desperate. Marcus texted back that he had no such luck reading

Mrs. Thronton's mind through his mother's. Admitting defeat to himself, Chase dressed in jeans that actually fit along with his favorite tee that read, "I speak Python." He laughed to himself as some thought his shirt meant he could speak to snakes, when really it was referring to the Python coding language. He looked through all the ties laid out on his bed, trying to make sure to pick the right one for the occasion. He grabbed the green-and-blue striped tie and threw it over his shoulder. This was the first time he actually felt a bit nervous about their presentation. He went to the bathroom, wet his curly hair, and then combed it. He was grateful that his dad taught him this trick for getting his hair to look somewhat tamed without too much pulling and tugging. After slipping on a pair of socks and tennis shoes, he headed for the door. His mother called after him, "See you in a couple hours, dear!"

The STEAM Chasers met in their classroom. Everyone was a bit disappointed that Chase couldn't get details on this big secret event from his mom, but they understood. They all thought their parents might have some idea, but none of them would tell them anything more than what Principal Davis had already announced to the class.

"Is this your first time back at the office since your scavenger hunt?" Terrence was curious how everyone felt about making a return trip and thought asking Chase made the most sense because his mother worked there.

"Yeah, I haven't been back yet," answered Chase.

"We decided not to tempt ourselves and make Shar angry." Marcus laughed.

"Well, it's a good thing I'm having such a positive influence on you two," answered Shar as she rolled her eyes. Her smile at Akiya let them know that she was only kidding.

"Well, I'm glad to see you two were able to show some restraint," said Ebony.

"You doubted us?" Marcus was trying to look serious, but that only lasted for a couple of seconds before he broke out laughing.

Mrs. Worthington was now standing at the front of the class. “Okay, everyone, gather round. Let’s get you all loaded on the bus. We don’t want to be late.” She managed to look both excited and nervous at the same time. They saw everyone pile onto the bus. Some projects looked to be quite extensive.

Now Akiya was feeling a little nervous, wondering how their project would compare to others. She forced herself to push that thought out of her mind. *Learning is a personal journey, not a competition.* She silently repeated the words that her grandmother told her whenever Akiya felt doubt about her academic performance. Her friends could never understand why she felt nervous at all, she knew more on some topics than some adults. However, Akiya was ever aware of all the things she didn’t know and constantly battled with everyone thinking she was the smartest kid they’d ever met, while she was frustrated that teaching herself differential equations was taking too long. She made herself breathe. Ebony sensed Akiya’s nervousness and gave her a smile. She then reached over and gave

Akiya's hand a squeeze. If anyone knew about wanting to be perfect academically, it was Ebony. They helped each other through these times of doubt often. They were the only two people they knew who would ask, "How much of an A is this A?" and they were probably the reason why the Global Academy stopped putting grades on most assignments!

Chase raised his hand and asked, "Is there anything we should know about this event before we go, Mrs. Worthington? You know—like who will be there, what they will be doing, why we are going to this particular spot to do our presentations in the first place? You know, the usual."

"You have all the information you need, Chase. I promise, this is all good. There is nothing to worry about. You all are getting a great opportunity to present all of your hard work to people who are interested in what you have to say. So, let's get started."

Mrs. Worthington shuffled out of the door. Regardless of how calm she was trying to appear, they could tell small changes from the way she normally presented herself. While Mrs. Worthington always wore slacks and a sweater or a nice blouse, today she was in a Global Academy blazer. She also had her hair pulled up into a neat bun. She even had on a shiny necklace. She was herself but a little more extra. It was clear she had taken a bit more interest in looking just right this morning. Their suspicions were confirmed when they saw Principal Davis. He was in a suit as usual, but he had a Global Academy patch on his lapel. He was also wearing a Global Academy tie. Akiya wasn't sure, but it seemed like he smiled extra wide as their group passed him to get on the bus.

It was actually a rare treat to ride the bus. Many of the kids were able to walk to school or their parents would drop them off. The buses at the school were usually reserved for field trips. The relief from Chase's thought ended quickly as they pulled into the parking lot of the Oxland Building. Terrence was the first to notice and he audibly gasped. This made everyone else turn toward the windows. Not only did the parking lot start to fill up with buses with other kids from Global Academy, there were also several police cars in the parking lot. Officers were getting out of their cars and heading to the building. They even saw Officer Carpenter and Officer Mitchell walk toward the building.

"Please tell me you two didn't go ahead with your plan," cried Shar as she looked at Marcus and Chase.

"We told you we didn't," said Chase.

"Honest!" said Marcus, who wasn't sure the group was convinced by Chase's answer alone.

Mrs. Worthington got to her feet as the bus came to a stop. "Okay, I guess the wait is over! Our big surprise is that we have all been invited to a special community celebration being hosted by our local police department. We all know a couple of officers got a wonderful introduction to our assignment by six of your classmates." Everyone turned to look at the STEAM Chasers. Terrence looked as if he was about to be sick again. Mrs. Worthington continued, "They were so impressed by what you all were doing, they wanted to do something special for everyone. We will hear more about it as we get off the bus. However, don't be too nervous—everyone is here to listen to your presentations, learn from you, and clap for you. You all have worked very hard, you're ready for this. Just pretend you are back in our classroom and talking to your friends."

With that, everyone started to file out of the bus. Chase couldn't even say a word, his mouth was just open. As he walked down the last step of the bus, he saw his dad waving at him. When his dad had his attention, he gave him their secret sign. It was something they'd made up when Chase was five years old and had gotten in trouble at school for taking apart a calculator. He remembered that he just wanted to see for himself what was making the numbers light up. When his dad walked into the building, as Chase sat in the principal's office, he thought his dad would be angry. Chase immediately began to cry. Mr. Thornton told the principal that he wanted to have a word with Chase before they started their meeting. Mr. Thornton took Chase to the bathroom. Chase started to cry even harder, thinking maybe his dad wanted to take him to the bathroom to yell at him or maybe tell him that he couldn't come back home and would have to live in the park from now on. No, his parents wouldn't make him live in a park. Maybe they would make him live in the backyard in a dog house or something like that. Of course, his parents had never threatened to kick him out of the house before and they rarely ever yelled, but Chase had never gotten into trouble like this before either.

When they walked into the bathroom, Mr. Thornton turned to Chase and said, "Son, stop crying. I know you were just being curious. I brought you in here so you would calm down and clean your face. Look, I'm on your side. They are right in that you shouldn't have taken apart a calculator that wasn't yours. I also know that you didn't do it to destroy it but because you were curious. You aren't in trouble, we will work this out. I promise." Chase had stopped crying but still felt unsure. "Okay, how can I show you that I have your back, even in the meeting?" asked Mr. Thornton. Chase shrugged his shoulders and looked at his shoes. "Eyes up, young man. Remember, you take the good with the bad with your head held up high."

Chase looked up at his dad. Chase balled his hand into a fist and smiled at his dad. His dad smiled back and balled his hand into a fist. Looking at each other, they banged their fists as if pounding a table and laughed. Chased had been called the Thunder since he and Marcus were toddlers. When he'd first heard about the comic book character—and apparently mythical god according to Ebony—he thought Thor was trying to steal his identity. But he liked that Thor had a hammer. Chase would run around with his imaginary hammer whenever he wanted to announce his entrance. At that moment, in that bathroom, all those years ago, that was the sign his dad would use to convey to him that he knew being a curious kid would sometimes mean Chase would cross a line—whether that was taking apart a calculator without permission or accidentally hacking into a government computer system.

It wasn't that Mr. Thornton didn't make Chase accountable for his shortcomings, he just made sure no one was allowed to define Chase by the times he slipped and ignored the good he did. In the principal's office that day, Mr. Thornton said Chase would buy a new calculator from his own money. He would also spend the weekend taking his own calculators apart and learning how they worked and have a presentation ready for his teacher and classmates on Monday. By the end of the year, even other teachers were coming to Chase asking him to fix their calculators if they stopped working. He wasn't known as the kid who broke calculators but the kid who fixed them. And that air-fist bump let him know that was what would happen with his father by his side. When Chase saw the fist bump, he realized his dad had worked his magic yet again.

As they all walked into the front of the building, they were surprised to be walked right out the side door, heading toward the grassy area Marcus and Chase would often use to fly drones. What greeted them was a huge sign saying, “Thanks for Being Our Neighbors!”

Chapter Fourteen

Officer Carpenter moved to the microphone. “We want to welcome everyone to our first annual neighbor gathering. It has come to our attention that maybe we don’t know our neighbors as much as we should. This is especially true of our youngest neighbors. We want to make sure they know they are welcomed throughout every part of our city, that their learning doesn’t have to be confined to their classroom, but this entire city is theirs to learn in and explore. We want them to know all of this is their neighborhood and they are welcome to enjoy it. We are going to start off with some presentations from Mrs. Worthington’s classroom. After that, we have a few other special awards and then we will get down to the business of playing together, eating together, and meeting each other as neighbors—not behind doors and windows but out in the open, talking, laughing, and shaking hands."

Marcus and Chase looked at each other. They could hardly believe it. The nosy person who called the police on them was being called out for being the one in the wrong. The entire community was backing the STEAM Chasers. Everyone was letting them know they were welcome there and everywhere in this community. Shar, Akiya, and Ebony were all hugging each other. Terrence looked to be in shock, followed by relief. He was drawn into a hug with Marcus and Chase. "We did it! Even without breaking the law," yelled Marcus, laughing. "I get to keep my drone license after all!"

It was fun to hear the presentations of the other groups. There was so much to learn. One group did a presentation on the influence of Black Americans on everyday life in areas such as general American culture like music, dance, and fashion. They showed how many forms of music derived from jazz, which was created in Black American communities in New Orleans in the 19th century. They clapped loudly as the group even demonstrated some break dancing moves, which is a dance genre created in in the early 1970s in predominately Black American communities and is currently being considered for an Olympic sport. Rebecca's group discussed the influence of Black Americans on language, dialect, sayings and slang commonly used in the United States today. Everyone in the audience was amazed that they had been using a Gullah word for most of their lives. The word "Kumbayah," which actually means "Come by here."

The group even taught the audience additional Gullah words. Rebecca beamed at Mrs. Worthington who was clapping so hard she could be heard over the rest of the crowd. Her pride in Rebecca and her team taking that one conversation and going far above what even she imagined at the time was showing through her face. Yet another team discussed Black Americans' impact on sports from basketball and football to golf and gymnastics. They looked at Chase as they noted that while Black Americans had not invented basketball, they had made a number of important adjustments to the game and were the catalyst for things such as Slam Dunk contests and Three Point Shootouts. Chase smiled, remembering his famous milk carton attempt. One team discussed Black Americans' impact on politics and the American political system. They even dressed up as politicians such as the first Black American female major party presidential candidate, Shirley Chisholm.

Finally, it was time for the STEAM Chasers. Chase walked up to the microphone, his knees shaking just a bit. "Good Morning, everyone. I would like to introduce you to the STEAM Chasers and our invention of the 'Am I Being Detained?' tie clip." Chase straightened his tie to show the metal device just under the knot. "We understand that everyone is aware of what happened to us a few weeks ago. We were lucky to meet officers like Officer Mitchell and Officer Carpenter. However, we thought about what could make experiences like these even safer for kids. Well, the first way to make them safer is for people not to call the police on a group of kids out doing their homework." Nervous laughter filled the room. Chase felt himself relax, just a bit.

"Our invention is based off of the things that we learned about what Black Americans have contributed to our everyday lives. For instance, we got the idea of having a camera based on what we learned about the video-linked security camera system patented by Marie Van Britton Brown and Albert Brown. Philip Downing's invention of the public mailbox inspired us to remember the importance of communication, so the device will send an automatic alert to a parent, guardian, or other loved one, letting them know where you are and that you are encountering a situation involving the police. William Wells Brown's book of *Clotel*, the first book published fiction book by a Black American, reminded us of the power of the written word. As a result, a transcript of the encounter will automatically be created and printed.

"Garrett Morgan's invention of the yellow light reminded us of the importance of slowing down and proceeding with caution. So, this device will send a message to the local police station that the officer is communicating with a minor and should be prepared to be patient and kind. The automatic sprinkler head system by Josepha Smith inspired us to ensure the device activates automatically at the beginning of the interaction.

Shar stepped forward and lifted her neck just slightly so the beautiful, stunning string around her neck would show. Chase handed her the microphone. "We know that not everyone wears ties. So we took inspiration from Nathanial Alexander's patent for the versatile folding chair and made the device also work as a pendant that can be worn as part of a necklace. John Lee Love's invention of the portable pencil sharpener helped us realize this device needed to be attractive and portable so that kids would have it whenever they needed it. Alexander Miles' invention of the automatic elevator doors reminded us that the device needed to improve safety, which is why we designed it to be worn high—away from the pockets. So if kids needed to activate the device, their hands would be moving up, not down, and their hands would be staying visible."

Shar paused as she saw a new aspect to the device she hadn't seen before. She turned to look at Chase, who shrugged his shoulders. Marcus walked up to the microphone. "With inspiration from the push rotary blade lawnmower by John Albert Burr, if you push this red button, it will summon a puppy army, currently in development. This should not be used for routine police encounters, but if you find yourself in the midst of a zombie apocalypse." Shar turned red. The audience started to laugh.

"Just kidding," said Marcus. "No puppy armies. "This button was inspired by John Albert Burr. When we used the push mower for ourselves, we found it was actually relaxing and calming. This button sends a signal to the officer and the adult being contacted, letting everyone know if the child is overly nervous, having an anxiety attack, or if the officer is successfully de-escalating the situation. Not everyone shows their fear on the outside. And for those who do, nausea from elevated anxiety levels could cause them to make a sudden movement as they turn to throw up. It will help everyone better to understand that kids in these encounters are experiencing fear and anxiety because they are just kids. We are just kids."

Shar was beaming along with the rest of the STEAM Chasers. They hadn't thought about the emotional aspect of the situation. Most of them almost ran, not away from the police but away from what they thought was a dangerous situation that didn't even concern them. Marcus had addressed the most important aspect of all—they were just kids. Kids get scared and in those moments they need the adults in the situation to step in and de-escalate, just as Officer Mitchell and Officer Carpenter had done.

The audience was clapping loudly. People even started cheering.

Chapter Fifteen

Soon, they saw several people heading up to the microphone. It was Officer Mitchell, Principal Davis, and Mr. Sparks. Also in tow were Mayor Shelia Salisbury and someone else they didn't know. Someone else was carrying a big rectangular sign of some sort. Mayor Salisbury took the microphone and got everyone's attention. "Those were all amazing presentations. Thank you so much for sharing! We all learned a great deal today. Let's make sure that our learning doesn't end here, for us adults or for the students. In fact, we are going to ensure that unique opportunities for learning continue to happen for everyone but particularly for one group of students."

Ebony looked at Akiya with her eyes wide open. She didn't know why she thought the mayor was talking about them. Something in her mind told her that she was right. The mayor continued, "Joining me today is Donald Oxland, owner of the Oxland Building we are standing in today. Please, say a few words."

Mr. Oxland took the microphone. "When I first heard about the experience six young people had a few weeks ago, I was disappointed. I wanted this building to feel like home to everyone in our community, especially such wonderful kids. I know some of them particularly well since they have family members who work in this building. I take great pleasure in watching two of these young men fly drones on our lawn early some Saturday mornings."

Marcus was turning beet red. He had no idea the owner of the building knew they were flying drones there. Shar gave him another "Good thing you didn't decide to go rogue" look. She didn't even have to speak the words, he could see it in her eyes.

Mr. Oxland continued, "It was an honor to have our building used to help build the bridges that may have been damaged earlier. However, I wondered if there was more that could be done. Officer Mitchell was wondering the same thing. And then we both started to get calls from others in the community who also wondered if there was more we could do. We asked Principal Davis to join us for this special presentation."

Chase thought he was going to burst. What in the world could be going on? He hoped they would all get to the point, he felt like he might be the one to vomit from anticipation this time. He looked for his dad. He was now standing next to Mr. Sparks. In fact, all of their parents were standing together by Mayor Salisbury.

Principal Davis began, "I would like to call to the front Shar, Terrence, Akiya, Ebony Marcus, and Chase. You all have greatly touched the heart of this community. You have helped us to examine ourselves and see what we can do to become better as neighbors.

One could say that you have helped us to reach higher heights so to speak." Mr. Davis let out a laugh. Ebony wondered if they were supposed to be in on the joke. He composed himself and continued. "Since you all have helped us to reach higher, we thought we would help you all reach higher—literally. So, your community has come together to send the six of you as high as we thought kids your age could go. We are sending you all to Space Camp!"

Shar was for the first time in her life speechless. She just froze with her mouth open.

Terrence thought he felt his knees buckling. He couldn't believe it.

Akiya pondered for a second if going to Space Camp was literally higher geographically or if it was simply a play on words. She pushed that from her mind and decided to just enjoy the moment.

Ebony had tears in her eyes. In her rooms, looking out her open windows through her telescope, she longed to learn even more about space. She had heard about Space Camp but didn't think she would ever have an opportunity to go.

Marcus started laughing. He always started laughing when he didn't know what else to do. His mind was racing.

Chase looked at his dad who was also looking back at him. How did he keep such a big secret? How did his mom and aunt and uncle keep such a big secret?

Principal Davis continued speaking, even though, for the STEAM Chasers, time seemed to stand still. "You have taught us so much about Black American contributions to our everyday lives, we can't wait to hear what you find out at Space Camp." With that, everyone began to clap and cheer.

Chase looked at Marcus and gave him a high five. Terrence joined in. Shar, Ebony, and Akiya hugged each other. Ebony's tears were flowing even harder. Everyone wanted this, but she wanted it so much more. This had been a dream of hers for a very long time.

"Are those happy or sad tears?" asked Marcus.

“Super, amazing, extraordinary, spectacular, wondrous tears!” said Ebony.

“Ebony is using so many adjectives she is going into Level Up Language over load!” said Marcus, laughing even more.

Shar jumped in. “Do you guys realize we have an official mission? We are going to find out about the blackness of space!”

Ebony was smiling from ear to ear. This was like a dream come true. All those hours of looking through her telescope in both of her bedrooms. She couldn’t believe it. She and all of her friends were going to Space Camp! Who knew that would happen when they decided to join forces for a homework assignment?

* * *